𝔐ythical 𝔗imes

Exploring Life, Love and Purpose
Maurice J. Turmel Ph.D.

Cover Art and Story Illustrations

Monica Yakiwchuk

Mythical Times
by
Maurice J. Turmel

Copyright 1996 by Maurice J. Turmel
Turmel Counselling Service
Winnipeg, Manitoba, Canada
Self-Actualization (Psychology)/Spiritual Life/New Age

Published by:

LightWing Publishing
Winnipeg, Manitoba, Canada

Canadian Cataloguing in Publication Data
Turmel, Maurice Joseph

      Mythical times: exploring life, love and purpose
      ISBN: 1-895292-73-5

1. Self-actualization (Psychology) 2. Spiritual life – New Age Movement.
I. Title.

BF637.S4T8 1995   158'.1   C95-920209-9

Printed and Produced in Canada by:
Centax Books, a Division of PrintWest Communications Ltd.
1150 Eighth Avenue, Regina, Saskatchewan, Canada S4R 1C9
(306) 525-2304 FAX: (306) 757-2439

What Readers Are Saying About
"𝔐ythical 𝔗imes"

Dr. Turmel's book "Mythical Times" renders with earnestness and clarity the individual's journey within, with all the engagement and power of Myth.

Dr. C. Jordan – Clinical Psychologist

I found "Mythical Times" to be an extremely useful tool to open up the imagination and take one on a journey into Soul. For me, little is more important than enlarging the imagination. Dr. Turmel's stories and poems provide a springboard for individual explorations of the worlds of the imaginal and as such they are precious gifts.

Per Brask – Professor of Theatre and Drama, The University of Winnipeg

After becoming aware of the drastic differences between the person I had become and my newly discovered Self, I was compelled to find guidance that would lead me to living my life as my Self - the person I was truly meant to be - instead of the person I'd become in order to simply survive. I found the guidance, and a way to access it, in a "Mythical Times" workshop. The use of mythical stories and guided meditations brought me to the place in my Self where my Soul lives. I have learned how to communicate with my Soul and now have the courage to accept the guidance that will help me to live as the person I was meant to be. And All Is Well in My World.

Audrey Birch – Insurance Systems Analyst

As a client of Maurice Turmel's I had the privilege of hearing the myths and poems from "Mythical Times" as they were being created. Whether read aloud by Dr. Turmel, used in his workshops, or appreciated in private, each one has relevancy for us all. They are like keys unlocking the mysteries within, helping to reveal ourselves and find our way to our longing Souls. A valuable guide for anyone on a spiritual journey.

Lois Galatiuk – Workplace Benefits Manager

The book "Mythical Times" takes one to a time of fancy, a place where solutions are possible. Put yourself into the characters' shoes and feel the ecstasy of success.

C. L. – Financial Analyst

After reading Maurice Turmel's book "Mythical Times" and attending his workshop, I would highly recommend this work to anyone seeking to integrate their life experiences with living symbols, emotional dynamics, relationship values and spiritual elements. This work provides a forum for the exploration of one's innermost being as well as an uncanny solidarity with the Universe and the external World. The short stories and symbols help the reader identify vicariously and compassionately with other elements of Creation - plants, animals, inanimate objects - and with the experience of one's fellow human beings. Dr. Turmel's creative imagination reaches the depth and core of one's experience of living, celebrating, and suffering and leads his reader to a new level of awareness, maturity, integration and solidarity. His writings are truly "Parables for Modern Times" which have a universal language regardless of one's spiritual or religious option. And they have the power to lead the reader within and touch the Soul and Its connection with the fullness of Life.

Reverend Gilbert Gariepy – Institutional Chaplain

I found the book "Mythical Times" fun and easy to read, and a great source of inspiration. I related to something in all the stories and gained many valuable insights from them. I have given several copies of the book to friends and family, who also enjoyed it, recommended it to many others and will continue to do so.

Dr. T. Michalyshyn – Chiropractor

All the stories in "Mythical Times" are an invitation – to discover the importance of having a purpose in life – to become conscious of the vital strengths within – in order to build self-confidence/self-esteem and become more autonomous. Each of us has the key to "All being well in her/his world!"

Amanda, Serving those who mourn – Funeral Chapel Support Services

While reading the book "Mythical Times" I am swept away from the logical, confining and predictable aspects of my everyday life. My imagination is awakened by the images of talking animals, wise characters and far away lands that exist in an unidentified place in time. As a result of being encouraged to allow my imagination to soar I feel great freedom and learn of my Self from the characters in the stories and the words of the poems.

'Audree' – Freelance Ghostwriter

Dr. Turmel's tales lead you on a journey within your SELF. You'll discover places on the way to your Soul you may have known were there, but never knew how to reach. Once there you begin to realize that the gifts you bring to this world are far more important than any material possessions you may gain while here.

D.L. – Accountant

This is a wonderfully uplifting approach to helping individuals come in touch with their spirituality. In seeking our true inner Selves, we search endlessly for guidance and encouragement. Maurice Turmel offers both of these in his book "Mythical Times" through the comforting and fascinating medium of stories and Myths. These are supported by illustrations that beautifully enhance the message and meaning throughout. I would recommend this book to each and every person who wishes to get in touch with his or her true and honest "Self".

K. J. – Composer

Dedication

" To Thine Own Self Be True" *
This Is Where The Heart Lies

With My Best Wishes
Maurice Lurruel

* William Shakespeare – *Hamlet*

7

Acknowledgements

I would like to acknowledge the following for their support and encouragement during the creation of this project.

My wife, Leslee, for letting me read to her on those many weekend mornings, for her love and for her encouragement.

All the members of my various therapy groups and the many clients I've had the privilege of working with over the years, for what they taught me about growth and change.

My good friend, Monica, for reaching down into her Soul to create the beautiful images that brought these stories to life.

Children everywhere, for what they continue to teach us about being open and alive and for expressing exactly what they feel when they feel it.

My friend Ken Johnson, for encouraging me to do the tape where my very first story was launched, and for his beautiful music and soundtrack that brought it all to life.

And finally, "The One Who Guides Us All", because of His/Her Inspiration, these stories now exist.

I thank you all for being in my life.

Maurice Turmel

From the Illustrator

The vision I carry of myself is merely a reflection of what I already know at a deeper level. The image I portray to the rest of the World is only a sampling of who I really am.

While modern science can claim to explain what I am, "Mythical Times" helps me to understand 'who' I am. The stories and poetry entwine with my inner Self, caressing, nudging, helping me to unfold, until the physicalness of my body is no longer a singular dimension. I am the grains of sand, I am the swirling water, I am the rush of air, I am the expansiveness of an unlimited Universe, complete, yet never ending. While my feet remain rooted to the ground, my whole being reaches out past unknown and undetermined boundaries, constantly growing like a thundercloud gathering force, until I am ready to burst forth and give back to my World the life giving nutrients I've gathered, pouring them all over the very ground I stand upon.

Maurice points the way toward the many paths I may choose to journey, and walks with me part of the way. The rest I find myself while realizing it is this guidance that leads me on to discovering my very own Soul. This guidance, I observe, is his gift of love, to be passed on and emerge through my unfoldment, to be passed on again and again.

Creating these images allowed me to enter my inner World and see through my Self the gifts of beauty and love that God intended for me to grow and express. These gifts I realize, were always meant to be shared and "Mythical Times" has given me a wonderful opportunity to do so. I sincerely hope you enjoy what I was able to bring forth here. They are my gifts to you from my deepest Self, and, from the very core of my being.

Monica Yakuwchuk

Table of Contents

Contents

Foreword

he myths of man have been with us throughout time. From the earliest of cave drawings to modern writing and film, mythical images and symbols have been a source of inspiration and guidance throughout human history. This has been the case, not only down through the ages but across cultures as well. Myths, as sources of inspiration and guidance, have been our teachers leading us through the various trials and tribulations that confront us as human beings. They inform, they guide and they teach. They help take us forward on our individual journeys through life. How else are we to find our way but through the images and experiences conveyed by myth in all of its varied forms? It would be a sad existence indeed if we were deprived of this most important resource.

Periodically, in our collective human journey, we have had major awakenings. Our history books inform us of this. All of our major disciplines are affected by this. A breakthrough in science often leads to a breakthrough in human awareness. For example, "the sun does not revolve around the earth" became the leading edge in the end of global self-centeredness. As a result of this information, we humans became part of something larger than ourselves, a part of the Universe if you will, rather than its center. When we take a collapsed view of our past, we can see that these awakenings have occurred regularly. Each epoch in human history has revealed this essential pattern.

With the information explosion of modern times we are likely on the threshold of another major awakening. The world becomes smaller by the minute as all of us aboard have easier access to our collective wisdom than at any other time in history. Our consciousness is uniting and with this we leave behind the individual isolationism of the past as we move toward the growing realization that we are indeed One.

In each epoch of history a symbol would emerge in the consciousness of man as a describer of this process at the individual level. The symbol for today is the arising of the Self. From Self-actualization to Self-empowerment, the symbol of the Self signals our growing understanding that at the center of us lies a core, and this core is our Self out of which emerges the expression of our truest nature.

This Self is not our Ego which has been our symbol of outward expression, and which now belongs to a dying era. The ego has been an integral part of the human journey to this point but is no longer its mainstay. It has been a stepping stone rather, into outward experience, and has brought us to this new threshold – the arising of the Self.

This Self contains that which we are at a primary feeling level. This feeling nature has been called Heart and sometimes Soul. Essentially it lies at the core of our being and describes who we are behind our masks and roles, behind all of our defenses. This Self is also, I believe, the same center of experience that is referred to in the "Recovery Movement" as "the lost inner child." As our center of unencumbered experience, this Self, when recovered, will then take us toward the next important step in our evolution, the greatest prize of all – our Soul.

Our Soul is our connection to all life and the very source of our being. Our Soul is of the Divine. It is that which imbues our being with meaning. At this point in human history it is time to actualize the Soul, to bring it forth into conscious awareness and recognize it as the true ground of our being. To actualize our Self is to actualize our Soul. The Soul, the Divine, the core of our being is from where we all came and to where we all return. It is Home, the final destination in this circular journey of 'separation – initiation – return'. It is the next chapter in a tale that has seen us move from a symbiotic relationship with nature, to separation from it in the development and evolution of the ego, to the return portion of the journey which brings us back to our natural source within. We leave Home to pursue adventure and growth. We return Home enriched by the experience and to celebrate that which we have gained. Our myths, our stories guide us out and bring us back again. They inform us of our lessons and alert us to dangers on the path. They reflect to us our experience in an easily accessible form. This is the very nature of myth – to inform, to guide and to explain, all in the simplest manner possible. And at the end of it all, when our journey is won, we can look back on our experiences and see them depicted in myth. Those simple little stories that say so much. They inspire, they guide and they touch. They help us open up. For after all, why else are we here, but to grow.

This book is about inspiration, about divine guidance and about the everlasting nature of the Soul. This book is also about the reality of "being", of one's purpose and of one's value. Each of us is truly a remarkable and gifted individual capable of synthesizing all that we need to inform and enhance our lives. This book lies in the tradition of classical inspira-

14

tion as has been handed down through the ages, all those powerful yet gentle reminders of the eternity of the Soul.

This book is about the Self, the awakening of the Self, the arising or surfacing of the Self and its relationship to the Soul. One's Self is not one's Soul. One's Self is only an aspect of the Soul which, in turn, is an aspect of the Divine Oneness. All life derives from that Oneness, which sees all and directs all. The Oneness governs life and informs each aspect of Itself of Its individual purpose in the Oneness. The Oneness is of course eternal, and exists beyond time and space as does one's Soul. The Self arises to meet the Soul which, in turn, brings it to the Divine Oneness.

The Self is brought forward and nurtured on the human plane of experience. The Self, in its ascent and ultimate expression, enhances the Soul. The Soul sees all and is all in Its relation to the Divine Oneness, that is, to Its particular aspect of the Oneness. But the Self is limited to the human plane of experience. The Self, however, does not disappear at the end of a lifetime as does the ego, but survives to merge with its Soul which it then enhances and enlarges. As already mentioned, the Soul, being eternal, is never lost, but neither is the Self. The two merge to become a greater aspect of the Oneness.

The Soul is why we are here. That is, we are here to learn lessons and to grow in order to enhance our Soul. There is no other reason to be here than to "grow". This is in fact the mainstay of our earth-bound experience. If one were to ponder this question of "why we are here?" for a very long time, there still would be no other conclusion. Earth life is for growth and growth is for the Soul. The Soul seeks out Life to expand Itself. Life presents It with opportunities for growth. *Growth is the reason for Life.*

This collection of stories and poetry is designed to help awaken that slumbering part of you. If you agree that your purpose here is to grow, then perhaps it will act as a mirror to your experience. Some of the stories will have more meaning for you than others. Some may have little meaning initially, but more meaning later on. Approach each story individually, as an opportunity to learn something about yourself. Look at each character and situation as a possible reflection of something going on in your life. Additionally, the characters themselves may reflect on different parts of your personality, giving you another view of your inner life. Let them speak to you and inform you of who you are. Let them touch you and awaken in you that which has been asleep. Trust that you will derive from them what you need. The stories, after all, are simply mirrors to your experience. Your experiences and how you feel about them will tell you who you are.

The stories in this book celebrate Life. They also celebrate accomplishment and, of course, growth. Each story, in some sense, celebrates coming to terms with one's Self, with knowing that Self and, with honoring that Self. And this process in turn leads us to our Soul. That is where we want to be – first with our Self and then, with our Soul.

I believe that the Soul was conceived in God's eyes as an extension of Itself. This God-energy determined that Souls would enable It to extend Itself and further Its own growth. God is truly an energy that feeds on Itself in order to grow. As an energy It casts itself about in all manner of forms that permit It to learn more about Itself. This energy appears to be voracious, having an enormous appetite for experience. Experience leads It both away from and back to Itself, returning richer and larger and wiser than when It first set out. God apparently sees no end to this process. All of Its creations are designed to further this primary purpose, which once again is to grow and expand.

Why God chose to create Souls may be a mystery to us, but is obviously no mystery to Itself that sees all and encompasses all. Souls are Its way of extending Itself into many areas of experience for learning and growth. God's purpose, simply put, is to grow.

This book then is about Souls and their journey through human life. A Soul's journey can be wide and varied and can take many forms. The human form is just one example. The spiritual form is another. The essence of a Soul is contained in all of Its endeavours. A Soul seeks out human life to sustain Itself while here, and then to expand and to grow. All Souls are on a journey of Self-Discovery in order to further Their purpose and enhance the goals of the Divine Oneness. This is my understanding of the process and I take full responsibility for this description.

How these stories come to me is something of a mystery. I believe that I tap into something larger than myself when I'm in the mood to write, and a story or poem comes to life as a result. I never consciously ruminate about a story prior to putting it down. Even in the midst of writing it I often don't know how it will end. I in a sense "receive" it and then polish it once its essential features are out. I feel blessed that they come to me in such a manner and believe that they are delivered to me through my Self from my

Soul. They are gifts which I feel the need to share in order to allow them to do what I believe they can do – inspire, guide and teach. I have used these stories in my work as a therapist, both with individuals and groups. I am always amazed and gratified to see what an impact they can have on those who hear them. They do serve as reference points to experiences and feelings for individuals on a growth and/or recovery path. They do stimulate, challenge and intrigue. All the stories in this book seem to accomplish this in their own unique way. And the accompanying poetry serves to enhance this process of awakening Self and Soul by bringing out the focus of the stories in a different form. Poetry is the music of the Soul we have been told and I do believe this to be true. Whatever moves us, touches us, inspires us or arouses us has at its core an unswerving capacity to ignite. That is the undisputable nature of myth.

I sincerely hope you enjoy and benefit from what is presented here and I wish you all the best on your journey.

Maurice Turmel

A Matter of Trust

ong ago in a far away land lived a princess in a castle. This princess was very unhappy. All who had mattered to her had been taken away leaving her feeling sad and lonely. She had nowhere to go and no one to turn to. She loved nature very much. Nature was her only friend. She would wander the gardens and the fields around the castle to be near the flowers and the bushes and the trees, to be close to the animals who came in from the forest nearby. Many animals in fact had already befriended her. She knew them all by name. There was Wilbur the goat, Christof the cat, Raoul the snowy owl, and Leona the friendly bear. There were many other creatures as well, but no people to speak of in her life. She lived with her uncle who was away much of the time, so she spent most of her days alone.

One day, while wandering in the gardens, she came upon a gentle deer.

"What is your name?" she asked.

"Anthony," replied the deer. "And what is your name?"

"Genevieve," she replied, "or Genie as I prefer to be called."

"Very well, Genie, I am very pleased to meet you."

"And I you," she replied.

Just then arrows whistled through air. Anthony was visibly upset.

"I must go" he said. "The hunters are coming and they do not care who they shoot or kill."

"Oh dear," said Genie, "then you must run and hide before they get too close."

And off ran Anthony, away from where the sounds had been heard.

Genie was sad about this situation. Why would someone want to harm such a beautiful creature? She did not understand, for she truly loved nature and in her mind there was nothing more beautiful. Birds and animals, trees and bushes, all were alive and all were wonderful to observe and enjoy. She went about her day and tried not to think about it anymore.

The next day she was in the yard again and Anthony came out from the bushes. He looked scared and tired.

"I have been running all night," he said. "The hunters were very close at hand. I am tired now and I need rest. Can you give me some water and some food perhaps?"

"Why of course," Genie replied, "I'll do so right away." And off she ran to retrieve what Anthony had requested.

Within moments of her leaving a hunter came out from the woods and aimed his bow at Anthony. The deer froze but was too tired to flee. He just looked at the hunter and sighed.

"I have no fight left," he said. "You have found me and I surely must die. For you are the hunter and I am the prey and I can no longer escape from you."

The hunter lowered his bow and made no move toward the deer. His attention was now focused elsewhere. He had noticed the beautiful girl carrying water and food moving toward the deer. Genie had not seen the hunter as she was preoccupied with her task of attending to Anthony's needs. As she approached, she noticed the hunter and let out a scream.

"Don't you hurt him," she yelled out. "Don't you dare. This poor creature has done nothing to you and you have no right to harm him."

"Who are you?" asked the hunter paying no heed to her statements. "Tell me who you are," he repeated.

"I am Genie," she replied, "and this is my Uncle's castle. All the creatures around here are my friends and I will allow no one to hurt any of my friends."

"I see," replied the hunter. "Then you must accept my apologies for trespassing. I had no idea this was your uncle's property."

Genie relaxed a little recognizing the sincerity in the man's voice. She looked at him closely and noticed that he was quite young.

"Who are you?" she asked.

"I am Oliver," he replied, "I live nearby on my father's estate. He taught me to hunt so that is what I do. Again, I mean you no harm and I apologize for intruding."

Anthony was no longer afraid for he could see that the hunter had become captivated with Genie. As the two of them continued to talk, Anthony withdrew toward the forest and made good his escape while he had the chance. Genie and Oliver continued to talk, learning of each other's lives and interests. As it turned out they had much in common, both having been raised alone and having no friends with whom to spend time. Genie learned that Oliver had no mother and rarely saw his father. Oliver learned that Genie was alone much of the time also. He had learned to hunt because that is what his family did for amusement. She had learned to care for the creatures of the forest by befriending them and learning their ways.

Genie soon realized that Oliver was much more alone than herself. She had friends and companions. She experienced warmth and love. Oliver had none of this. He was truly isolated and his hunting prevented his getting close to anyone or anything. She invited him to visit her again but without his weapons. There was to be no more hunting on her uncle's grounds. He agreed and was greatly pleased with the invitation. He had not known anyone quite like this before and was happy for the opportunity to visit again.

And so it appears that Genie had made another friend from the forest. Another frightened, lonely creature had come forward to befriend her. She felt happy inside. Her world was not so lonely after all. Her gifts were trust and faith. She feared no one and believed the best about all whom she met. Oliver was a fine fellow she thought, just scared that was all. She had been scared like that herself not so long ago. She had feared to venture into the world and discover its beauty and warmth. But bit by bit she had learned to trust, learned to reach out, learned that others would respond to her openness with warmth and openness in return. Whatever she gave out came back to her tenfold. For every smile she offered, she in turn received hundreds. For every caring gesture, she was rewarded with friendship. How could she be lonely with all this abundance? She realized that her gift was to touch others and they in turn would touch her too.

As she returned to the castle that evening she felt blessed. She had made a new friend and she had learned something valuable about herself. She had much to give and equally much to receive and for which to give thanks. She hadn't before realized how truly fortunate she was until she saw the loneliness in Oliver's eyes. Yes it was true the two of them were alone much of the time but she had befriended the creatures of the forest, the plants and the trees. All were her friends and she theirs as well. All lived in harmony in her world which, since Oliver's arrival, had now grown just a little larger. She was truly happy and she gave thanks.

And All Was Well in Her World.

A Land Far Away

nce there was a young man named Maury who lived in a faraway land that few had ever visited. This land was populated with all manner of strange creatures and bizarre landscapes. Trees grew to be two-hundred feet tall and creatures never seen anywhere before roamed its mysterious woods. There were no rivers or streams to speak of, however, there were regular showers from heaven above to water the plants and provide sustenance for all the creatures who lived there. Some of these creatures had two heads, others three tails. Some were large and ugly, some were smaller and more attractive. But all were unique. These creatures came in all sizes, shapes and colors. No one color, size or shape prevailed.

All the creatures in this strange wooded area lived in relative harmony until one day when a stranger arrived in their midst. This stranger had very unusual manners and ways of communicating and dealing with the creatures of this forest. He would yell at them to get out of his way or push them or intimidate them with his great variety of weapons. He was a very unhappy man. He had been banned from his own homeland by his neighbors and friends because of how poorly he treated all of them. He had become angry and surly over the years as a result, it was thought, of having lost his wife, who died of a terrible illness. Until that time he had been a reasonably nice man just given to periodic outbursts of temper. All this unpleasantness went by unnoticed though since most of the time he was reasonably pleasant and friendly.

When the man's wife eventually died of that very rare disease, it was then that he became more surly and distrustful. He yelled at or attacked anyone who came near him and eventually upset all the people in his home area. They finally had enough and agreed to have him banished from their land. So when the decision was made a group of the villagers brought him to this place where Maury and the creatures of this forest lived. The villagers did not know who or what resided in these strange woods. They felt that by leaving him here they would be well rid of this man whom in their eyes had become intolerably obnoxious and impossible to bear.

When the stranger first arrived he was not surprisingly even more angry than ever. He cursed and he swore and he threatened vengeance on his former villagers. He was very bitter and very angry. The creatures in this wooded area did not remember seeing anything like him before. They had become used to Maury who seemed to have always been there and treated them with respect and loyalty. They in turn respected him and honored him even though he was as different from them as they were from each other.

So when this strange angry man appeared, the creatures of this land became quite distraught. They were not used to being yelled at, or attacked or threatened in any manner and they weren't sure how to handle this. Many of them felt feelings that they'd never felt before - hurt, anger, rage, upset - all very unpleasant feelings with which they were at a loss as to how to cope. A delegation of creatures was sent to fetch Maury in order to help them deal with this intruder. "Should we kick him out?" some of them asked. "Should we physically remove him?" another group wanted to know. "What should we do?" they all said in unison.

When the delegation arrived at Maury's home, they were all excited and speaking at once. "A strange man has come into our midst. He is sour and surly. He upsets us very much. He hurts us and calls us names. We want to be rid of him. Help us get rid of him" they all cried out. Maury listened intently and proceeded to acknowledge their distress. He told them he could see their hurt and upset and he could understand why they wanted to be rid of the surly man. But he had another plan. He explained that these behaviors they were describing he had seen elsewhere and thought that this situation could be handled in a more productive way than by just casting out this unruly intruder. He suggested that all the creatures go off to their homes and dress in their finest celebration attire and then meet him at the place where the man was last seen.

"What we require is a celebration," he told them, "rather than a condemnation. We need to celebrate because a lost soul has found his way to us and, rather than reject him, we should welcome him in our usual friendly manner."

"We," he went on to say, "can continue to be our happy selves if we choose to and see how he responds to us then. We already know how we respond to him and his outbursts of temper."

So off all the creatures went to gather up their finest attire and to rejoin each other in the clearing where the stranger had been sitting on this day. As they approached the area the man jumped up and started yelling again. Maury motioned for all to stay calm and to continue to approach cautiously. The man yelled louder and began to make threatening gestures. The group continued to approach slowly. Maury stepped forward and greeted the man.

"Greetings, sir. Welcome to our forest. How may we help you?"

"By leaving me alone," the man yelled back.

"I see, sir," Maury went on. "You wish to be alone. But we of the forest invite you to join us in our celebration."

"What celebration?" the man grumbled.

"Well, when a new creature arrives in our midst we all gather and wear our finest attire to welcome him and make him feel at home."

"Why would you do that?" the man asked?

"Because we all have been lost at one time or another sir, because we all have felt rejected and afraid and because we all have felt angry about something and needed to yell at life in return."

"Well, for such a strange group you seem to know quite a lot about people who are not from here. How is it that you know how I feel?" the man asked.

"Because," Maury replied, "the others and I have felt the same at one time or another. Look closely at us. Are we not odd? Are we not rather unusual? Are we not the strangest bunch of creatures you have ever seen?"

"Yes," the man replied. "Now that I look at you all, you are indeed a strange looking group."

"And that is why we live here," Maury continued, "because no one in the world out there accepted us as we were. If we did not conform, if we did not appear acceptable to their standards, we were driven away. And eventually, we wound up here."

"So how did you get to be so friendly?" the man asked.

"Well, in the early days we were not so friendly. We also yelled and screamed and threatened each other at first. But then one day we began to talk with each other about how we came here and about our losses and hurts, about our feelings of pain and rejection, and then we started to feel better. We then made it a practice to talk with each other regularly and to talk to new arrivals as soon as they came. But it's been so long since we have had a new arrival that we had forgotten how to behave. We had forgotten our own losses so we didn't recognize you at first. But now, as you can see, we do and we wish to welcome you among us."

The man looked dumfounded; he was sad and happy at the same time. He recognized that he was welcome and he acknowledged their kindness. He asked them why they were so friendly when he in fact had been so rude. He went on to say that he had never experienced this level of acceptance and friendship even when things were good in his life. He admitted that his big hurt began when his wife died, but that there had been hurt there before this tragic event. He was so pleased to see how accepting all these creatures were that he now wanted to share everything about himself. Something in the air here made him want to do this. He was grateful for the opportunity to express himself and to share. In all his life he had never felt listened to and, as a result, he had become bitter and surly. Now that he could speak, he felt greatly relieved and hoped that he could be forgiven for his earlier rude behavior. Maury then stepped forward to formally accept his apology and began to share with him some of the basic premises that were at work in this strange land.

"First, we acknowledge and value all life forms. We make no distinctions and place no greater priority for one over another. All are important and all form the fabric of our existence. We have learned that we need each other. What one can't do, another can and so on. We have come to realize and appreciate this."

"Second, all creatures, great or small, require Love. There is no exception to this rule. We believe that even the rocks need love and we make it a priority to provide each other with that basic need."

"Third, we value each other's uniqueness. In this great diversity are we strong and capable. Because we are so different we can help each other in many unique ways. We have done great things here because of this wide diversity of individuals and needs. Our diversity is our strength. In the outside world, the world of conformity, our distinctive features were often considered aberrant and were condemned. Most of us were banished from there because of our unique but unusual features or capabilities. In this realm, where cooperation reigns, we recognize these differences and we value them. Our view is that there is strength in diversity and what others have rejected, we have determined and proven to be of great value. There is no waste here. A creature with three tails can swat more flies than with one tail. A creature with two heads can carry on multiple conversations and look in two directions at once. A two–hundred–foot tree provides little shade, but can easily peer into the distance and advise of incoming weather patterns, the migrations of birds and other creatures and the approach of strangers. Everyone has a function, everything has value. Even an angry, surly man like you can have value if we can help you get through your pain."

"Fourth, we believe that all creatures, all persons, all living things are basically good. And we believe that a surly man is angry because of pain rather than as a function of character or disposition. We have yet to be proven wrong in our approach. And you, sir, are the latest proof. For a while there many of us forgot this basic premise but since we remembered and proceeded to welcome you as we did we learned once again that our basic premises were correct. Now you sir can join us if you wish and share with us your vast experience and wealth of knowledge. We feel blessed by your arrival and celebrate your turning about on your former anger. Will you join us then and share what you know?"

"I will," the man replied, "and I thank you for receiving me so warmly. You are truly an incredible group of creatures and I thank you all for your warmth and generosity. Please let me repay you in any way I can by offering whatever manner of talents or abilities that I may have that may be useful to this beautiful and unique place."

And a resounding "cheer" was heard far and wide as all the creatures of this "land faraway" rejoiced at the man's words. Another lost soul had been salvaged from himself and his former pain and losses. Another beautiful being from God the Creator was beginning to flower once again after so long laying fallow. This man, who was now born anew, exemplified his new freedom by beginning to express himself from within, and as a result of this new found self-appreciation and self-expression, his pain began to heal and he began to thrive once again.

And All Was Well in His World.

Fallen Angel

Once there was a young man named Phillip who considered himself to be a gallant and noble gentleman. He loved to attend gala events and to promote himself as a keeper of profound and important information. He fancied himself to be quite a ladies' man, a raconteur and noble gentleman even though he had no noble lineage of which to speak. He actually came from poor stock and, so, was determined, at a very young age, to rise above his meager circumstances and travel in the company of nobility and upper class society.

Phillip had no idea at the time of his excursion into high society that he was giving up his Soul, those special basic values that had sustained him throughout childhood, and that he set aside so he could meet his goal of travelling and living within these higher strata. He found he had to cheat and to lie and to misrepresent himself constantly in order to gain acceptance and approval from those whom he so ardently admired and aspired to emulate. For their part, these members of the so–called "elite" had little interest in Phillip, only to the extent that he might be useful and, therefore, to only momentary advantage. Other than that he was considered a pest really, a simple irritant who had gained some measure of notoriety that could be used occasionally for someone's ulterior purpose. Phillip had no idea that he was held in such low regard. His vision of himself had him quite elevated and, in his own mind, he saw himself as well received and as having achieved his goal of recognition and acceptance in this world of the elite.

One day, when Phillip was again trying to impress yet another group of upper class individuals, he came upon a woman who captivated him immediately. Phillip did not notice at the time but, at the very moment of this encounter, all about him had come to a standstill. The people he had been talking to were frozen in time, while he, unaware, continued to fix his gaze upon this resplendent creature who now totally held his attention. While he stood there transfixed the woman, who was now staring him right in the eye, began to speak.

"You, sir, are a thief. You are a scoundrel and a ne'er-do-well. You do not belong in this society. And you do not deserve the recognition that you are seeking here. You are simply a phony. Not because you were born into lesser circumstances, but simply because you misrepresent who you actually are. You are not true to your Self. Therefore, you are not a truly noble person."

Phillip was dumbfounded, he could not speak; he could not answer; he could only stare in stunned silence. This woman saw right through him. Who was she to be so perceptive? How did she happen to be here on this day? And why had she chosen to challenge him in full view of these individuals he was trying so hard to impress?

The woman looked at him with an eerie smile. "Look closely at me Phillip. Do you not recognize me? I AM YOUR SOUL! I am here to remind you of who you are. I have come to you today to disarm you and to alert you to the danger that you have imposed upon yourself. You are at great risk of losing your Self forever. These external circumstances are not who you are. They are simply a distraction, a trick of mirrors designed to betray you and lead you astray. You have only one task in life and that is to find your True Self. There is no other purpose. There is no other need. You wander around in this plane getting yourself into all kinds of mischief, believing that your purpose is here or there, believing that you need this or that, believing that you are so special as to be excluded from the normal fate of man. You are deluded, my friend. You are as lost as ever despite your fancy clothes and your polished banter. Does anyone really know you? Has anyone really seen your deepest Self? Have you looked inward lately to review your life and yourself within it? Then you cannot be truly satisfied no matter how hard you try as you are living a lie. Where is your truth Phillip? Where is it? Is it in these games you play? Is it in these little deceptions you designed to gain you access to these so-called elite worlds that you convinced yourself are so important? Where are your close ties? Who loves you Phillip, other than me? Who indeed knows you well enough to love you? No, my friend. You have wandered down a blind alley. There is no virtue here; there is no love; there is no salvation. In pursuing these goals you have in fact moved "away" from your Self, not "toward" your Self. You are not expressing your true Self. You are instead expressing some unmet need from your past and you are trying to fill it externally rather than through your inner being. You believe that these so-called special people, these noble ones and their privileged circumstances have something to offer you, and can bring you satisfaction. Has this yet happened? Has your gnawing, inner need, been met?"

Phillip had to turn away, to avert his eyes. He could no longer look at this woman who had unmasked him and posed so many questions that went straight to the core of his Being. She had challenged him. She had undressed him. He was awash in shame. He had indeed abandoned himself.

"You are a fallen angel," she went on to say. "You have simply lost your way. Come with me now and we will see if we can restore your life to a healthier state. Forget everything you have taught yourself to this point, for you have deluded yourself with all manner of falsehoods. First of all, there is no outer world to speak of, only a mirror to your inner experience. If you feel lost in the outer world it is simply because you are disconnected from your Self on the inside. Secondly, there is no purpose to life except to arrange circumstances to cast the most favorable light on your Self, so that it can more easily be found and restored to its true place, at the center your being. This Self of yours is all that you are. Everything else is just window dressing, props for the great drama of life. How easily does one become blind to this? How easily does one forget it seems? Not so long ago, when you were a child, you reveled in the glory and wonder of nature. Your Self was who you were then, pure and simple. Then you lost sight of that primal reality as the outer world began to take up more of your energy and attention. You soon began to pursue what you thought were worthy goals out in the world and you misplaced your Self in the process. Now here you are, alone in life, living in the circumstances that you most admired, and trying to believe that you are happy and actually have what you want. Yet you have no companion or partner with whom to share. Your only lover is your illusion which needs daily reinforcement lest it crumble before your eyes, much as it did today when I appeared before you and confronted you. You see how fragile an illusion can be? But then your Self, your inner light as it were, is unshakable because it knows and lives only one truth, and that truth is derived from all Eternity and from your Divine center. Only in this special place at the core of your being can you truly say – I AM – and be accurate in the most fundamental sense.

There you have it, my dear Phillip, your sacred Soul is here returned to you in such a manner as to awaken you to whom you truly are. You may go on with your illusion or you may take this Self that is your Divine birthright and go forth and express it to the best of your ability. Know this and know this forever. There can be no substitute for the truth of whom you are – no distraction – no replacement. This Self who you are is not replaceable and it is up to you to honor it and bring it forth. Do you understand me, my dear friend? Do you understand how important this is? Then go forth and honor that which you are. You have no other task."

31

With that said the woman vanished and Phillip was left to ponder his thoughts and reexamine his life circumstances. A call had been issued, a powerful but loving admonishment, and yet a gentle reminder to awaken and be true. Phillip now knew it was all up to him. He had two paths in front of him and much more information than at the beginning of this day. What was he to do now if he wanted to ensure:

That All Would Be Well in His World

There really is no use pretending. The Lord is here. He has put out a call to all who will listen. The word is simple, He has a need to see us. He says He's been lonely and is eager for our return. "Find your Selves," He says, "and listen closely, for the rhythm of the heart will lead you there. But past that point, you'll find your Soul waiting. Meet with Self and Soul as often as you can. They connect you to Me. And from here, We can command that future you wish to grow, which is to be found here. All it needs is your determined push and it will begin unfolding."

Don't hesitate any longer. Don't hold back your sweet gifts. Let them out, they are needed. Give them back to Him!

Open Your Heart

here once was a woman named Giselle who lived in a small village near a mountain range. Here creatures of all kinds roamed freely. This woman's husband had died and she was left widowed. Since his death Giselle had lost her taste for life. No one who knew her had much to do with her anymore. She had become old and bitter and had taken to wandering the streets of her village all alone and without concern for those who would come upon her.

She seemed to be in a daze most of the time. Her children had grown up and left home. They could not tolerate her insensitivity toward them and her inability to express any warmth at all. To them she had died also when their father passed away. They had become emotional orphans left to fend for themselves and to provide each other with what little comfort they could.

Giselle had drifted from all who had once meant so much to her. She had lost her children and what friends she once had. She had also lost her capacity to enjoy nature and the beauty that surrounded her native village in its magnificent mountain setting. Her heart had turned to stone some said. Others thought she had simply lost her mind. In her isolation she had withdrawn from all who once held such importance to her. Eventually she could no longer tolerate any closeness to anyone and moved away from the village into the nearby hills. She now resided in a sparsely maintained hut located in an area where only a few wild creatures roamed and occasionally wandered near her property. The villagers avoided this area since Giselle was known to be so withdrawn and unapproachable. They all left her alone now, as did her children, and as did all who came to know her story.

One day a beautiful golden eagle soared overhead, very close to Giselle's home, looking for food as eagles were want to do. Some scraps that had been tossed outside caught the eagle's attention and it swooped down to gather them up and have itself a long overdue meal. Just as the eagle landed and began to feast on the scraps Giselle came out of her hut and let out a scream. She had become so used to being alone now that she rarely expected to see any creature in her yard. The golden eagle, sitting there eating scraps of food, had really startled her and she was at a loss as to what to do. The two of them stared at each other for a few moments before the eagle sprang up and let out a screech of his own.

"Who are you?" he asked.

"I am Giselle," she replied. "This is my home and those are my scraps of food that you are eating."

"I see," replied the eagle. "I apologize for the intrusion. As I flew over this area, I noticed no one around and assumed that it was deserted. When I saw the scraps of food I decided to land and have something to eat. When you came out of your hut, you startled me, much as I startled you it would seem."

Yes, they were both startled it appears, neither one of them expecting to run into the other.

Just then another creature approached the area from the hillside nearby. It was a large horned goat and it was quite curious about all this noise and activity.

"What's going on here?" the goat asked. "I was minding my own business, eating grass up above, when I heard all this commotion, so I came to investigate."

"And very well you did," the eagle replied, "for this lady lives here alone and I startled her. I am very much remorseful over this as I do not intend to upset anyone during my travels. You are her friend perhaps?"

"No, I am not," replied the goat. "But I see her every day, tending to her chores, going about her affairs here all alone. I noticed that no one comes to visit, that she is always alone and so it surprises me to see you here."

"I understand," the eagle replied. "This lady is not known for sharing company so my presence here seems quite unusual."

"That is correct," the goat went on. "At any rate I see that all is well and I will return to my grassy area above and resume my grazing."

Just then a thundering sound was heard coming from far off in the distance. It sounded very much like horses that were fast approaching. Giselle was visibly distressed. She had not heard the sound of approaching horses in years and became quite frightened as to what threat this might pose. The eagle volunteered to fly up into sky and survey the area to see what indeed was the source of this thundering sound. As he soared over-head he noticed there were in fact many horses with riders aboard but they were not coming in this particular direction. Instead they were headed at a threatening pace toward the village. The riders were armed and ap-peared to be quite menacing. They wore fierce expressions of grim determination like men who were going into battle. This could only mean that the village was their goal and the villagers would obviously be unaware of this impending attack.

When the eagle returned to Giselle's hut, he informed her and the goat of what he had seen. The three of them began discussing what to do. The goat volunteered to run into the village and warn them but the eagle said "No." The villagers would not likely listen to a goat. And nor would they listen to an eagle the goat suggested, for birds of prey were not considered friendly. It was left to Giselle to decide what to do. She had never felt so frightened before. She had never felt so helpless. If neither the goat nor the eagle could help the villagers, then who could? She had not spoken to the villagers in so long that she feared they would not listen to her or even allow her to come near them at all.

Just then an angel came to call and descended upon the area of Giselle's home with great grace and calm. The angel looked at Giselle and spoke. "Look into your heart, my dear woman, where you have been asleep for so long. Look into your Self and find the words and phrases that you need. You can do this. There once was a time when you could express yourself and readily be heard. There once was a time when all that mattered to you came easily to the surface and you shared it with those you loved and for whom you cared. Remove that stone from your heart and find once again that place within where Love and Caring flow. Reach down inside and touch that space and go forth and share what you know to be necessary."

Without any further thought to her own safety or to the consequences of her actions, Giselle raced toward the village shouting at the top of her voice "The warriors are coming. The warriors are coming." The villagers were quite startled as they had not heard this woman's voice in many years. They gathered round as she approached and became concerned at the level of her agitation. They listened intently as she reported what she had heard and what the eagle had seen. The thundering sound was growing louder so all could hear now and know that Giselle spoke the truth. Arrangements were quickly made to rally the village defenses and soon all were prepared for the approaching danger.

When the band of warriors came close to the village, they quickly realized that it was well defended. Having lost the element of surprise they decided not to engage in a costly battle and chose instead to move on. The threat passed and all soon returned to normal again in the village. It very quickly became apparent to everyone that Giselle was responsible for saving the town. The villagers wanted to thank her but were concerned about making such a gesture given Giselle's long held reluctance to have anything to do with them. A child came forth and volunteered to deliver their message of thanks. When the child and a number of villagers arrived at Giselle's hut, she received them warmly and accepted their expressions of gratitude. She had tea with the delegation and visited for a while before the group returned home to report their success.

After that it became widely known that Giselle was open to visitors. In fact it became quite a fashion to saunter up the mountainside and spend time with her. She had become a gracious hostess and she seemed eager now to share time with all who came by. The eagle and the goat were regular visitors too, along with a growing number of individuals from the village. Giselle had awakened from her deep somber sleep. She had reconnected with that vibrant vital part of herself that could express warmth and love. She was no longer alone now as she had rediscovered friendship and sharing. Her eagle friend and neighbor goat were her family now and the villagers her friends. She had found that place in her heart where Love dwells. She had to be frightened it seems to get there but when she did she relighted that feeling with all her strength into a very bright flame. She was at peace now and grateful with the knowledge that she could feel again and that she could express what she felt. And because she could feel and express what was in her heart she felt alive and eager to share in life and all its joys.

And All Was Well in Her World

Imagine if you will a vast pool of water. In it you find all manner of aquatic life, some of it microcosmic, some of it larger than life, all of it derived from one source, the 'He' who guides us all. Into this water He poured all the contents necessary to construct life – the amino acids, the circulatory systems, the bone marrow and the flesh. The mixture was complete and the Sun took over the final stages. In no time at all there was life burgeoning forth on this plane, the everlasting life that continues to thrive to this very day. Put yourself into that context. This is where you came from, and to where you will return. But not before you've experienced every aspect of this life. The microcosmic and the cosmic, all part of the grand design. See yourself there. See your Self now!

Oh Soul Delight

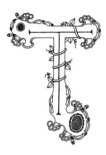he spirit of this song is the night, the time when Souls ascend, when creatures rest, when bodies sleep. This is the time for spirit, for essence, and for upliftment, when the moon can be an image for the Soul, and when this song can be a call to Its awakening.

1st verse:
    Oh moon above, how can you see
      The light of all eternity
      There all alone, and all aglow
      Are you still seeking where shadows go?

      Into the night your sweet embrace
      Takes me forward to that special place
      Where hearts aglow and spirits fine
      Soar beyond limits to the ends of time

Chorus:
    Thou art so great
    Thou art so fine
    Take me to thy bosom
    Till the end of time

2nd verse:
    As shadows fall across my room
      I visit again that pale-hearted moon
      Drifting across the inky night
      Till dawn returns with its full flight

      My heart ascends, my Soul sublime
      Seeks out your wonders to the end of time
      I am here now to experience all this
      Your wonderful glow, your eternal bliss

Chorus:
    Thou art so great
    Thou art so fine
    Take me to thy bosom
    Till the end of time

Bridge:	And when you speak your whispers dear To help me unfold and be with you near You are my Soul to soar forever You are my Heart and none so better
3rd verse:	When daylight comes and wakes me again Shall I be stronger than when night began? Oh lonely night, you take me far Out into flight, my Soul to soar And now I know why my Heart aches For your sweet look and sweet embrace I love you truly my Soul delight You are my angel come through the night
Chorus:	Thou art so great Thou art so fine Take me to thy bosom Till the end of time
Close:	As daytime shadows fall across the land I find my Soul is in my hand To guide me forth toward one more night And take me again on another flight

We had never before imagined how grand life could be, till we found ourselves at the bottom of a pool, made of mud and water, filled with promise and love, mixed by 'Him who guides', sent from Heaven above. No, we couldn't see past our daylight hours into the dark of night where sleepy shadows would draw out their might. There in the darkness, out of the mists of time, came a life force so powerful you just had to make it your own. Now you are on the threshold of another great leap forward. See yourself in this context and watch your Self unfold.

A Call to Your Soul

ometimes our Soul can be lost in a state of isolation and pain. Because It has been injured, It may be reluctant to come out, to rise to the surface. But It does want to come forth. By your invitation It can. Simply ask It to be there, to rise and meet you on the surface of your life. Perhaps this prayer will help.

Be there my lost lonesome part of me
Be there and tell me what you need
I cannot allow you to stay hidden any longer
I need you and beseech you to come forward

You are my friend and lover
Where have you been?
I have missed you and now I seek you
To join me in my life and to share with me
To rejoice, to celebrate and to heal
Where have you been my dear one - I need you?

Please come forward and greet me as I greet you
You are my Soul sublime
Where you are, so am I
Whatever you need I will provide

Come forth my angel from the dark
Come forth and join me on this quest
Without you I can go no further
Without you I too am lost
Come forth my angel from the dark
Come forth and greet me
So we can be together again

I feel sad that we have been apart for so long
I feel sad that we have not been together for a time
I know we do not know each other well
But I believe we can overcome that

Please come forward so I can meet You
And we will see what we can be together

Oh Soul Delight II

Oh Soul Delight
You are so dear to me
You are so fine
Take me to thy bosom
Till the end of time

An Ode to your Soul. Is it not a sweet gesture, an inviting gesture, beckoning forth that part of you that has lain dormant for centuries? Can you feel its pull on your Heart? Can you not feel the tenderness within? The Love? Yes, the sweet Love? As you invite and affirm, your Soul draws near and taps you on the shoulder in answer to your prayer. The song in the earlier chapter is a prayer and a prayer is an invitation. None so powerful as a song of prayer, beckoning forth that which lies dormant and asleep, while awaiting its call, its invitation to soar, to rise and take its place at the center of your being.

And again:
Rise oh Soul . . . Rise up and expand within me . . . Fill me up with your presence, my Soul Delight . . . Do not keep me waiting any longer . . . Come to me now, I need you, I want you . . . Come to me now . . .

And again:
You are my Soul Delight
Come to me through shadows of the night
Come to me now and let us take flight
Let us soar to the heavens above

You are my angel come out of the night
Whisper to me softly, your tales of the Light
I am your shadow awakening to your sound
I am here on Earth where your spirit abounds

Come to me now my Soul Delight
Come to me out of that sweet dark night
Soar with me upwards into God's gentle Light
Soar with me forever my Soul Delight

As shadows fall across the land
I am so happy, you hold my hand
And take me forward to that special place
Where I can enjoy your sweet embrace

You have captured my Heart, my imagination too
I am your lover as would be true
Do not let me die without your touch
I need your presence so very much

Come to me now my Soul Delight
Come to me out of that sweet dark night
Soar with me upwards into God's gentle Light
Soar with me forever my Soul Delight

I am once again captivated by your face
I feel you in my arms, your sweet embrace
Thank you once again for coming to me "dear"
I take you into my Heart, to hold forever near

Come to me now my Soul Delight
Come to me out of that sweet dark night
Soar with me upwards into God's gentle Light
Soar with me forever my Soul Delight

On wings of love and ventures told
We seek our destinies
Shone in the stars and reflected back
To help us off our knees

This tale we live and share with all
Is a path we are never sure of
But ghosts along the way, we know
Will help us to take care of

All perks and props and seasons' lore
That keep us inward staring
Our center we call 'love', it seems
Has need of our preparing

To meet the One who stares from out
Our centers and our feelings
He has our Souls in His fair hands
He has us as His greetings

Thus we know where we belong
Catch a train this morning
Outward bound we sing our song
And meet you at the station

The place where all these hearts they go
To get their information
To learn about their lot in life
To help Him build a Nation

The Wizard

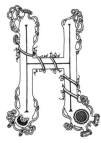igh atop a mountain lived a strange and grizzly old man. He was a fortune teller and a trickster, given to manipulating events to suit his own purposes. This old man had a daughter named Genevieve whom he called Genie, and whom he loved dearly. She was his whole life and without her he would surely feel empty and alone. Nordof, our craggy old man, was given to many flights of fancy. Some of these could be real, others occurring strictly in his own mind. He would spend days dreaming of tricks he could play and occasionally he had opportunities to act out his schemes.

The local gentry loved to invite him to their gala events as he was sure to amuse and intrigue. On one occasion he appeared as an eagle and flew about the ballroom to the great delight of his hosts. On another occasion he appeared as a wolf and growled and howled frightening many of those present. But it was all part of the game and he knew that to be invited to these events he would continuously have to change into one form or another with each illusion being more daring and more surprising than the one before.

His daughter Genie loved him very much. She was the only one who saw him as the real person he was. She knew he was lonely, but that he always feared exposure, and preferred to appear as a creature than ever show his true Self. An occasion of extreme importance was about to take place and Genie and her father were both invited to attend. Nordof, of course, was expected to perform and Genie was along for company and to assist in the evening's festivities. As it was, the neighboring gentry was also invited to this affair as there was to be a wedding between a local family and one from that nearby community. A young man and a young woman had been betrothed since childhood and now these two very important families were to come together through this marriage. Of all events of recent date this was to be the most fabulous and the most grand – unmatched some said by any event in local history. And Nordof, true to form, was expected to provide his most unusual magic at the behest of his hosts – all to celebrate the merging of these two families and to impress the neighboring gentry who knew little of his legendary wizardry.

As the big day drew forth, Nordof became increasingly agitated. His daughter was concerned. She had not seen him like this before. Usually her father cackled with glee at the thought of the tricks he was concocting. But not this time. He shared little of his discomfort with her, but continued to appear visibly unsettled. And so as the day of the gala wedding approached Genie became more concerned.

Nordof was up in his room on the eve of the event trying to concoct the greatest trick of his illustrious career. Much depended on his performance as his tricks were always the mainstays of any event in this particular region. And as many important personages would be travelling from great distances to attend this event, it was all the more important to achieve something memorable for this noble gathering.

As Nordof stood in frustration looking out his castle window, a thought came to mind as no other he had ever had. Why not just appear as himself, dressed in his favorite garb and present to the gathering the one thing no one besides his daughter had ever seen – his true Self. Nordof was dumbstruck at the idea. That was it, the coup of his career. No one would expect it, no one would even recognize him, least of all the gentry of this locality. As the thought settled in and became his emerging focus Nordof took stock of himself and was pleased with his plan. He shared it with no one, not even his daughter, for all were to be surprised on that special day.

The guests arrived from far and wide filling the ballroom of the host family's fine home. The neighboring gentry was all adorned in their most lavish of costumes. The locals were equally well dressed. Nordof and his daughter were to arrive later and the guests were soon abuzz wondering what trickery he might present. As the evening's festivities progressed, some agitation was noted as the wizard had not yet arrived. "Do not fear," someone said. "It is all part of his usual preparations for something of a grand design."

Just before midnight Nordof arrived with his daughter in tow. He was dressed in his finest costume and wore his most notable jewelry, totally resplendent in his attire and appearance. His daughter was equally well presented and adorned in her finest of costumes. The guests all looked in their direction waiting with great anticipation to see what would happen. But nothing outlandish occurred. Nordof went into the gathering, greeting all he knew and saying hello to those guests who he recognized had travelled far for this event. The hosts became impatient and approached him.

"What trick are you going to play this evening?" they asked. "When will it take place? The guests are growing impatient," they went on.

"And impatient they should be," Nordof replied. "Why are they here? To be amused or titillated? Those days are gone for me now," he went on. "As I reflected on this evening's festivities and my place in them, it came to me that I am tired of being something I am not. I am tired of transforming myself into something grotesque or bizarre for the amusement of others. Are your lives so boring that you need a trickster to add excitement? Is it not sufficient that two groups of people have come together to celebrate a wedding?   Is that in itself not sufficiently important that there must still be a need to overshadow this with some shallow trickery?"

The whole room had come to a standstill as Nordof explained himself. The hosts were stunned. They felt chastised and shamed. The other guests were equally stunned. Who was this old man to criticize their need for frivolity? And then someone exclaimed: "Oh good for you Nordof. You have fooled us once again. We were expecting the unique and the bizarre and you strike us from a different direction altogether. Bravo! My good man. Bravo! Once again you have outdone yourself. We were waiting for a grand and magnificent spectacle and you fooled us with this straightforward presentation. You surely have outdone yourself once again."

It was Nordof's turn to be taken aback. He was coming forth as naturally as he could and his actions were interpreted as part of his usual cleverness. He was truly sad and had not expected this at all. The crowd by now had resumed their merrymaking, chatting amongst themselves and laughing with delight at how clever this trickster was. "Imagine," some were heard to say, "the cleverness it took to come up with such a simple plan." Who could anticipate what Nordof would do next? He was a wizard after all and no one could predict his next move.

As the merriment carried on, and the hosts returned to their guests, Genie came over to her father and looked into his face.

"I know what you were doing, Father. I know that you were sincere. They are used to thinking of you as a trickster and only in that way can they be comfortable in your presence. But I know you in many more ways, including this one and I know you were sincere."

Nordof and his daughter left at that point for there was no reason to stay. He had accomplished his mission even if no one else noticed. They were all so certain he could only be one way. But then again, that's the way it was in their lives.

As time went on there were other gala events but Nordof was not invited. It was no longer fashionable to parade such trickery around and most hosts were uncertain now as to whether Nordof was really a wizard and prankster any longer since that fateful night of the wedding. Nordof and his daughter carried on with their lives. She met and married a fine young man who came to know Nordof as the man he truly was. And others did too as word spread around of his radical departure from his old ways. Nordof himself was also pleased at his change in direction. He was proud that he presented his true Self on that particular night even if no one really noticed or understood. He knew he had been sincere as did his daughter. And now many others know him as he truly is. With those thoughts, he felt blessed and reassured.

And All Was Well in His World.

Secrets spell that special place
Where all are kept at bay
Away from where our hearts do tell
What love is ours today

More than that they offer us
A simple way of safekeeping
That imprint He wrote for us
And placed it on a key ring

Now it hangs from round our necks
And says "I'm yours far after
Open up that case of yours
And let out your true Master"

You never know what lurks in there
Unless you untie knots
But keys will work so much better
And let out secrets, lots

These private thoughts and feelings too
Are yours to be protected
But if you let them out in time
Then Heaven will be wrested

The Discussion

There are several entities gathered this day. They've travelled from far and wide, from the furthest reaches of the galaxy, to participate in a most important discussion. While standing near the doorway of the meeting room one can easily overhear the dialogue being spoken within.

There is a large table at the center of the room. The entities, now seated, begin their discussion on a matter of extreme importance. The subject at hand is "The Right to Be." A chairperson opens the dialogue with a statement of assumptions and the following question:

"Does 'the family of man' as we know them have a basic right to be given their record in the history of human affairs?"

"You, sir, are a fool. No man has a right to be unless that right is granted by God. The human entity is a poor example of God's greatness. How could one be so foolish as to actually believe that these human entities deserve further contemplation or support? They are extremely selfish and nonfunctioning in the basic sense of furthering God's work."

"Yes, but do we not have a need to allow these creatures to awaken to their individual and collective destinies and thus their true identity?"

"We have waited for eons for this group to graduate. Look at how slowly they react to their spiritual essence. So many of them do not understand themselves. They wallow in fear and in pity. What can we do to accelerate this process of awakening?"

"I, for one, am tired of waiting. These creatures are quite silly and quite foolish. They continue to avoid responsibility for themselves and to violate the basic precept of all life forms, which is to honor each other's 'Right to Be'."

"I agree on this point. They are foolhardy and backward. They lack the necessary character and will to appreciate the interrelationship of all life forms and, without such respect, they are always at risk of destroying each other. How can they graduate to the next level of evolution if they cannot appreciate this simple fact? All life is interrelated and anything they do to another life form they ultimately do to themselves."

"This is all true, but some among them are awakening. These will be the leaders and 'way-show-ers' of their future. With enough of these individuals interspersed throughout the race it is possible that the general awakening we know is necessary can still happen in time to meet the Earth's next cosmic shift."

"Right you are. A great number of these entities are in fact awakening right now. And as each Light turns itself on, the way is shown for many more to follow and to achieve that same status for themselves. We must be patient lest we too become so discouraged as to miss this important opportunity to observe one of the greatest shifts in human consciousness to occur in several millenniums. This is no small feat, this awakening process, as we can readily observe from our vantage point here in the heavens. Each individual has to struggle with their life to find that center of their being, their Self, and then come to appreciate, at a core level, the inference behind the precept 'The Right to Be'."

"This is an excellent point. Of what value is this discovery of Self if it is simply handed over from Us to Them? To be won through one's own diligence and perseverance is a great achievement and testimony, through each individual who reaches that understanding, of the race's capability of finding its own way Home."

"We have been away from this struggle for too long ourselves and have forgotten what a challenge it can be. There was a time when we too fought our way through obstacles, limitations, fears and disabilities, to learn the lessons of Life. 'The Right to Be' is sacred and cannot be controlled externally. It is not our responsibility to impose our standards on a race whose only reference points, at the moment, are each other and the occasional advanced 'light' among them who takes them further on their evolutionary march."

"I for one would question the presumed authority we might claim to judge or to dictate to this group of entities. It is true they can be destructive. It is also true that so many of them are still asleep. But the Awakening has to proceed at its own pace and without interference lest 'We' violate the precept of an individual's 'Right to Be'. 'You be You' and 'I'll be Me' is the basic precept of any individual's 'Right to Be'."

"We are all in agreement then. Their pace is slow and their lessons tedious, but nevertheless, they have this basic right and they need to find their own way through growth into freedom. Let us adjourn then until further notice and await their next move. With so many of them awakening at this time it seems almost inevitable that the massive shift we've been awaiting will take place on its own accord. Let us retire from this discussion and allow human history to unfold as it will. We can observe, but we must not interfere. We can assist, but we cannot inject ourselves into their process. It must happen of its own accord and within the guidelines of noninterference prescribed by 'All-That-Is'. The God of Love oversees all. Let us trust that 'Its' presence is at work here as well."

And so the meeting adjourns and the various delegates return to their respective spheres of experience. Some we can see are solely Light entities, while others appear to have some physical characteristics. All hail from differing parts of the Universe. Yet all share a common goal – the further expression of All-That-Is and the protection and advancement of every entity's Self and sacred "Right to Be."

A Message

All is not lost, my fellow humans, for I am of the Divine and I wish to inform you that there is a great plan afoot and much to rejoice about. Do not fear for God is near, nearer than you may realize. Let there be no doubt that this is so. For I have spoken to you down through the ages, through your great ones who translated my thoughts into words and then into books. Your bible is one such thought as were many of your classically inspired writings given to you by the great ones of your race. Do not despair, my fragile ones, for I have come to you this day to advise you of wonderful news. You are indeed whole. You are indeed free. You are indeed holy. Take these thoughts into your heart and know that this is true. For I have spoken, and I speak only the truth.

There was a time long ago when you could not hear my words at all. When you thought that all there was to life was survival. You ran with the beasts then, unknowingly, unaware of My Presence in your circumstances. You were frightened, lost and scared. Many of you feel that way today - once again - frightened, lost and scared. Your systems of government are failing you, your scientists are failing you. No one seems to have answers of any substance. You delve into alcohol and drugs for relief. You belittle yourselves. You live in despair, all the while forsaking that which could truly set you free – Your Self – Your Innermost Being, that part of you that binds you to all life and from which you derive your primary sustenance. I have not betrayed you. I have not deserted you. You have lost and abandoned your Selves. This has been your error, my dear ones, for I, the God of Love, would never abandon My seed. I reside in each and every one of you. Some of you can hear Me, some of you cannot. Some of you can feel Me, most do not. It is you who have lost Me and not the other way around. I am the truest and most consistent experience in your life. Throughout your history I have been there, breathing into each and every one of you, guiding you and proclaiming your true nature. Sometimes you heard Me, sometimes not. Throughout history I have had to remind you, again and again, of your true nature and My presence within it.

Do you want to hear the story of the Fall? I will share it with you once again. In the beginning there was a void, a vastness of unknowing, a lack of form. The God of Love, Who I am, wanted to create an experience of "knowing," an experience of "appreciation" where He/She could realize themselves and see themselves evolve. The inspiration came to create a

61

being in My likeness who would reflect my greatest qualities and who would give these form in an area of experience that could be deemed visible. And there you were born my special ones, by Divine decree. By My word you were brought to life. You were spirit then and only spirit. You had not form as you know it today, only essence. But that essence was magnificent. How proud I was of my creations. You became fruitful and multiplied because that is a characteristic with which you were endowed by Me. You created each other then, replenishing, as it were, the Divine spark through each other.

This process as was created continued for some time until one day some of you decided that you wanted more power to create and replenish yourselves. And so it was granted. The power to create and duplicate yourselves was passed over to you exclusively, to use wisely I hoped, but to use freely nevertheless. My greatest gift to you was your freedom. I set you free to create as you would. And you did so honor Me. Then came a time when some of you came forth and demanded more power, the power to control others, the power to manipulate and to deceive. There was no thought on My part to extend this to you, but you took it anyway because your freedom, which had already been granted, justly permitted it. I was distraught of course, but could only observe since you were free to act as you would. I watched you perpetrate various horrors on each other, all in the name of experimentation. I watched you hurt and judge each other in the name of the good and the holy. You continued in this manner for a time, not knowing really how you were hurting each other and, therefore, your Selves.

Then I decided to make form from essence and I chose to extend the experiment into the visible, out of the void, into that in which spiritual essence could be made manifest. In your world that form is human, born of a spiritual essence. This humanness is just a distraction, a plaything if you wish, for you to see and experience your lessons with each other. At some point this essence, which became form, forgot itself, forgot its origins. All the while the plan carried on as you exercised on each other your various experiments and lessons. And these are still going on today. Your callousness, your manipulations and other atrocities continue to be perpetrated on each other in the name of learning, when really, while in your hands, it has always been about power – those of you who want more, those of you who want less. Your appetite for power has fueled your greed, and this desire to be greater than that which created you has been at the root of your fall.

And that, my dear ones, is the Story of the Fall. You were great, you were beautiful, you were grand in all manners. But you lost your Selves in your hurry to conquer or avoid being conquered. No matter what you believed you had won, you had in fact Lost. There is never anything to be gained by conquering another. You are all the same. You are all equal, equal to Me in fact and you are all One. What purpose has all this experimentation served? To teach yourselves limits, boundaries, healthy interaction, sharing, love, truth and justice - all your great precepts, which so many of you violate and treat with disdain. So where does that leave you now? On the brink of destruction? Perhaps. On the brink of discovery? Perhaps also.

I am here to remind you of Who you are, Who you Really are. And you are all much more than you realize. The experiment failed. There is no greater power than the Self and Its Divine inheritance. There is no greater truth than that which I offer. There is no greater reward than that which leads you back to your Self, to your own true nature, to your Divine essence and right to be. I plead with you, my dear ones, to awaken to this truth. You are Divine and you are Eternal. You are of the everlasting Light. Do not deceive yourselves into believing otherwise. There is no other truth. There is no other reality. I am the Truth. I am the Way. I am the Path. Find your Selves now. That is your destiny and that is your freedom.

Go forth in Peace and in Love.

And All Will Be Well in Your World

A Prayer

Oh Lord above I look to You
For sweet surrender and sweet embrace

I seek Your face in all that I do
I seek Your wonder so that I may come true

I know I beseech You to come forth from the night
I now seek Your Love in all that I delight

My heart leaps for joy when comforted by You
My Soul sings Your praises in everything I do

I came to be instructed, to absorb all I could
I came to rejoice in matter and learn what I should

My heart guides me forward and takes me to that place
Where I can feel Your heartbeat and look into Your face

I'm not saddened by what life brings, only intent upon my chore
To learn all I can from Love and beg You show me more

I love to let my heart sing with Your presence so fine
I am happy to open myself up and let my Soul shine

This effort I make on your behalf is simple and is true
I come to life as Your sweet thought to do what I can do

And when You wish for me return I will speed my way along
For I have done all that I could in Your "Forever Song"

The Sad Man

t was a sad day after all. The man had just lost all of his wealth and his family too. He awoke that morning in the midst of loneliness and despair. He had nowhere to go, no one to talk to, nothing to look forward to. These were tough times indeed.

There had been better days not so long ago. A successful business, a happy family, and many gifts and rewards flowing his way. But something different happened on that fateful night, something that changed his life forever.

If we look back now, we can retrace those steps. In his younger days our man Anton was given to fighting and arguing and pushing his way through to gain what he wanted. His temper cost him dearly in those early days. The losses were immeasurable; the failed relationships were many. Anton could not fathom it at the time. His father had conducted himself similarly, and his mother had acquiesced. So why wouldn't this style work for him?

As Anton learned to push his way through with his father's ways, he became even more subtle in setting out to attain his ends. He learned to cajole, to manipulate, to embarrass, to essentially transform a resistance into something more pliable which in turn allowed him to gain his way.

The woman Anton married was won over in that fashion. It was not a union based on Love and Respect, but on need, his need to have a mate and have power over that person. When the children arrived, the pattern carried on. No one was allowed to be their true Self, as Anton wouldn't permit it. He had to have control and to reach that end he would do anything.

As his business grew and prosperity reigned, Anton felt proud of his accomplishments. His family appeared well, his friends seemed admiring. But his employees feared him as did most of his neighbors. He was too powerful they said, not a man to get close to, much too conservative, much too purposeful, much too demanding.

And then one day it happened, the unthinkable, the unbelievable. A small rebellion had been brewing in the hearts of his wife and children. They had been cajoled and manipulated enough. All their cries for true intimacy had gone unanswered, their pleas for compassion unheard, and their needs for closeness unmet. Anton was not to be swayed. His formula for life had worked thus far he believed and he was not prepared to abandon it now. But then, upon arriving home one day, he found a note. "I am gone forever," it began, "and have taken the children with me. You are not to trouble us or pursue us in any way. We want peace, we want affection, none of which has ever been available from you."

Anton was devastated. At first rage swept through him like a violent storm. This soon gave way to sadness and finally, to grief. What had happened? He could not fathom it. He tried to carry on with his life, but his efforts were without spirit or design. His business began to fail and soon others left him – employees, friends, even acquaintances. Anton was now alone. He had failed he thought. His father's formula for life was in disarray. He could not understand what had gone wrong.

While he sat there, desolate and despairing, an angel came to offer him comfort and solace.

"What can you do for me?" he asked. "I am a broken man. I have lost everything. I have no worth. I have failed with my life."

"Tis true" replied the angel "that all about you has collapsed. But are you certain you have lost everything? Are you certain there is not some important remnant for you to take away from all this?"

"I do not understand what you mean," Anton replied. "I just told you I have lost everything, my family, what few friends I had, my business – my life really. I have nothing left, can you not see that?"

"I can see that externally you have lost a great deal," reflected the angel. "All those things that you thought mattered have vanished, this is true. But, are you not left with something, something you may not have noticed before. Underneath your father's shadow, underneath your family and friends, underneath all that you once valued, is there not a spark that still glows, that still sustains you, that still gives you life?"

"What do you mean?" Anton asked, now curious as to the angel's perspective.

"Well," the angel replied, "in the heart of every living creature lies a spark, a bit of the Divine fire, the fuel and energy that animate all life, including yours. Have you not noticed that in the realms where externals are not so important there is still laughter and joy? People with very little enjoy good humor, good fellowship, appreciation of their lives and experiences. If this exists for them as separate from external circumstances, could this not also exist then for you?"

"You mean at the core of my being lies hope, lies drive, lies determination which then can be transformed into all manner of external appearances?" inquired Anton.

"Why yes, that is exactly what I mean," the angel went on. "Some have called it Soul. Some have called it Self. Some have called it Spirit. Some have called it by many other names. But by only one name is it constant and true and that name is 'Heart' – the heart of love, the heart of being, the heart of full manifest expression. All other experiences return to this central point – your Heart and Soul, the very core of your being."

"I see," Anton replied. "So if I still have my Heart, my Soul, my Self, I am not destitute, nor a failure. I can recreate anew. I can express my Self in new ways. I can go forth and rediscover life from this most blissful and powerful of centers. I am not lost, I am free. I am not broken, I am whole. I am not without worth, I am valuable. I understand this. It makes sense to me now. How can I thank you for showing me my core and my indisputable value?"

"Express it," the angel said soundly. "Express that core to the best of your ability. Wrap yourself in Love and respect everyone's need to express themselves. As a representative of the Divine Creator whose essence animates all life, your task is to express that which is you and to share with others that which you have learned. Go forth and make yourself proud again. You are worthy and you are healed because you are willing to heal your Self."

And so Anton did. And so it was from that time on:

That All Was Well in His World

My '95

The Trickster

here once was a young man named Martin who lived in a castle in a far off land. In this castle many strange things seemed to occur. Walls appeared to move and furniture sometimes changed shape, magically of course and without prompting, or so it would seem.

Martin loved this castle. It was his home. No one else lived there at this time but Martin never feared being alone for he had many ways to amuse himself. He would imagine a certain shape to something and "voila" it would happen. For example, if he wanted a chair to become a table, he would simply imagine it and it happened - the chair was now a table. If he wanted a lamp to become a chair, the same thing would happen again, as soon as he imagined it. Martin had no end of amusing himself with such activities. When strangers came to visit, he would delight in tricking them with his amazing abilities, and they in turn would be left scratching their heads wondering if what they had just seen was, in fact, real. One minute they might be sitting in a chair chatting away with their host, the next minute they could find themselves on the floor rolled up in a rug, with no idea how that happened. Martin would chuckle with glee at his mischievous pranks. Oh how he loved to trick people and delighted in their inevitable dismay.

One day a beautiful young woman came to visit. She had heard of Martin's notorious pranks and wanted to see for herself the kind of mischief of which he was capable. When she came to the door, Martin greeted her with a handkerchief in hand, which he then quickly transformed into an umbrella. The young woman took the umbrella, examined it closely, and then returned it to Martin as a handkerchief, leaving him standing dumfounded at the door to his home. Collecting himself Martin invited her into the castle and then quickly proceeded with more of his usual trickery. But no matter what prank he played, the young woman would reverse it immediately so that there was never any real impact made upon her. Martin was becoming frustrated very quickly. As he led her about the castle, playing prank after prank, she continued with her own practice of reversing all of his efforts. After a time Martin stopped trying altogether and proceeded to ask her what she was doing.

"I am merely countering all of your foolishness," she replied. "I am not here to play games with you. I am here to visit with you and get to know you. But you seem more interested in playing your little pranks. I know you can do all these amazing things and I have no doubt that you are extremely gifted. But what kind of person you are is what I want to know. What do you think? How do you feel? What do you value? These are the things I am interested in knowing. So tell me, who is this person behind all these abilities? Show me that face and I will be truly impressed."

Martin was dumbfounded once again. Here he was facing a person he could not impress with his pranks, a person he could not trick, a person he could not manipulate. She saw right through him and could counter any move he attempted to make. His tricks were of no concern to her. She wanted to know who he was. "What to do?" he thought. "What am I to do?" Suddenly he came up with an amazing plan. "I will imagine the bravest, most handsome, most successful man I can and then present that image to her." And so he proceeded to imagine this magnificent being in order to transform himself into that image. Just as he was about to change himself into the vision he had created, the young woman stepped up to him and looked him straight in the eye.

"Not your visions do I want," she boldly stated. "Not some artifacts from your imagination, but you, sir, from the depths of your Soul do I want to see, the very essence and core of your being. If you can show me that face, I will lead you to a great treasure, never before seen, never before discovered, never before appreciated by anyone."

And so Martin pondered her words and decided to try again. This time, in his imagination, he went inward and asked that all his resources be brought to bear on this task of bringing out his true Self, his ultimate essence, from the very core of his being. And it happened! There before him, in his mind's eye, he could finally see his Soul, his beautiful, golden, pristine, exquisite, brightly glowing Soul. And the young woman was pleased. She did not counter his efforts this time, nor did she interrupt his process as it unfolded before her. She merely stood there in awe at the beauty taking shape and then thanked Martin for showing her who he truly was.

Martin was most pleased with himself. Finally he was able to distract her from countering his every move. Finally he was able to hold all of her attention as he had always been able to with all the other people who had come by previously. He was pleased with himself and felt in control again. Now he wanted his reward.

"So where is my treasure?" he asked. "I wish to see my treasure now," he quickly repeated.

And the young woman smiled as she prepared to answer.

"Where is your treasure you ask? Why it is right here before you my dear friend. You have blessed me with a view of your beautiful golden Soul, the greatest treasure of all. Your very essence, holiest of the holy, highest of the high, divine unto Thee, and unto Thee totally free."

She paused then to let the full impact of her words wash over Martin. Then continuing she added, "You are truly a God, sir, which means you are far more than a mere trickster. A God is eminently more capable than any master of illusion. A God is "whole" unto Itself, needs no distractions to take away from that Self, needs no external power, control or illusion to confuse Its inner being. A God is complete, and complete It remains, throughout all eternity. You have just shown me your treasure, your beautiful golden Self. Do you still have need of your illusions?"

Martin hung his head. He knew she was right. He knew she had seen his essence. He knew that this was far more important than any game he could play, or any of his tricks, pranks or illusions. When he revealed his true Self, there was no longer any illusion, only simple, pristine beauty that was his treasure and his life. He thanked her for the lesson and he thanked her for the help in returning him to his life. She bowed graciously and then quietly slipped away. Her task was done. Another Soul had been found and reclaimed for all time. Another individual had come out of the darkness of illusion, into the Light of day – the Light everlasting, the Light of God within.

And so Martin returned to his castle life, but there were no illusions now, no more tricks. He would just be himself and enjoy getting to know that person. For he, too, was a son of God, born to this life to radiate his true Self. And with that thought he felt happy.

And All Was Well in His World.

An Inward Journey

here once was a man named Arthur who lived in a land where only creatures roamed. He had come there, from a far off place, to be alone with himself and to journey inward where he believed his Soul truly dwelled. Arthur had grown weary of life's daily demands, of the need to please others, to gain his bread at the expense of his Soul. He had journeyed all around the world to find that special place where he knew he could go inward and find his Soul for the very first time.

On one of his journeys out into the world Arthur had met a Wizard who had taught him the art of meditation. On another journey he had encountered a Goddess who had taught him to listen to the rhythm of his heart. And on another occasion he had met a child who loved to play and sing and, therefore, taught him to be his natural Self. Now that he had left the outer world behind, he wanted to bring all of these lessons to bear on this inward journey to his Soul. He chose this isolated place so as not to be distracted and wanted all his attention focused on this very important inward quest.

On this particular day, as he was preparing to journey inward, a beautiful bird flew by, fluttering its wings and creating a great disturbance. Arthur waited until it left and then resumed his preparations for his journey inward. As he was once again getting comfortable, a small furry creature scurried by making much noise and creating yet another distraction. Arthur patiently waited until the creature had passed and then resumed once again his special preparations.

Arthur was just about to begin again when some dark gloomy clouds rolled in and the sound of thunder was heard from off in the distance. Soon lightning was flashing all about and rain poured down heavily as the storm moved through the area. Again Arthur waited patiently feeling certain he was being tested but not understanding why. The storm eventually passed and the sun came out soon after and once again Arthur went on with his preparations.

No sooner was he in the best of possible moods than an elephant came roaring through the woods very nearly trampling Arthur in the process. With his heart in his throat he tried hard to regain his composure.

Eventually settling down, he once again turned his attention toward his preparations.

This time there was no disturbance, no noisy creatures, no sounds of stirring from the woods, no wind, no rain, no thunder, absolutely no distractions of any sort. Arthur descended into himself and entered a labyrinth of crystalline colors with lovely bright hues, glowing and dancing and tingling his imagination. At the center of all this glowing delight was a bright reflective gem which beckoned him forth and announced Itself as his Soul. Arthur stood transfixed before Its awesome beauty. He remained still as he stared and drank the whole scene in. The bright gem then began to address him.

"What is your wish?"It asked.

"I wish to be with you," Arthur replied, "my bright luminous Soul. That is why I came on this quest. That is why I prepared so diligently. That is why I waited so patiently for those external distractions to stop."

"I see," the gem spoke. "So when I came to you as a bird you thought it was a disturbance and waited till I flew away. And when I came to you as a rustling furry creature, again you waited for me to pass. And then later, as a storm, you let me roll by once again unheeded. I thought if I charged you as an elephant perhaps that would get your attention. But no, once again you waited. So I decided to wait for you here. I prepared this room filled with all these bright twinkling gems with their beautiful colors and hues and then cast myself into the shape of this large jewel. Then you took notice. Of course you had some predetermined idea how I might look, so here I am meeting those expectations."

"You mean," Arthur asked, "that you have been near me all along and I kept missing you repeatedly?"

"Yes, you did," the jewel replied. "I come in many forms and in many ways to greet and advise you of my presence. I take many shapes along the way, give off a variety of perfumes and make many different sounds including 'roaring' with an elephant's gusto, depending on what mood I am in. It's up to you to take notice. When you have your mind set on a particular shape or circumstance then you will likely miss the thousand-and-one other forms that I may have taken. After all as your Soul, your connection to the Divine, I am as capable as He in manifesting myself into all sorts of disguises. What you perceive as a tree could be Me casting shadows for a small creature in the grass. What you imagine is a lake may be Me embracing all manner of aquatic life. What you conceive as the Sun is perhaps Me again projecting Myself into the outer atmosphere of the planet to warm it and provide light. I can be all of these and more as the many mirrors of your inner life for which you have quested.

Your journey is not to find the perfect formula for meditation and inward contemplation. You must 'feel' and 'experience' yourself to the fullest and then you will see me everywhere, in every creature, in every person, and in every event of your life. For as your personal Sun I radiate to you from everywhere, not just from within. Do you understand, my friend? Do you truly grasp what I am?

"I am your Soul, alive and bright and glowing in all things. Do not look for me in only special places as you will miss me again and again. Even in the tiniest specks of sand I may be found. When you look for me, look everywhere. And even when you are not looking I am there. For I am your Soul, your Forever Friend, your gift from God, here to guide and teach you and help you unfold into that most magnificent of beings of which you are. Now return to the surface my dear friend and notice what goes on around you. You are a sacred being in a sacred place, here to discover yourself in the face of everything you encounter. Do not miss a bird or any other creature for I may send an elephant once again to awaken you."

And so Arthur awakened from his trance to revel in all that was around him. This time he noticed the bird flying overhead and the small furry creature as it quickly scurried by. Now he didn't need the storm, nor the charging elephant to gain his attention. For he was now awake and alert and he quickly observed that everything around him had a special glow which he had not previously noticed. All life was sacred he remembered, as was he.

And so Arthur left this isolated land to return to the life he had before. But this time he noticed and drank it all in, and he truly appreciated the wonder of it all. That special glow was with him now as he was awakening to his Inner Light. And with that in mind he felt truly grateful.

And All Was Well in His World

Soul Searching

ou are embarking on an Ocean Voyage. The seas are calm. The sky is blue. A slight mist is blowing in off the water. Your ship is fully provisioned, ready for the journey ahead.

As you prepare to leave, news comes of a far-off disaster. You are alarmed, you are upset, you are concerned. And then a song comes to mind, a song you have heard many times, a song that has soothed you before, that has touched your Soul and alerted you to dangers within.

This song is a call to arms, to awaken you to your true Self. This song is a beacon for you to follow on your journey Home. For Home is where you wish to be at this time. The news of the far-off disaster alerts you to this, forewarns you of impending doom and, therefore, the need to move on with your life.

You sit on the shore by your small vessel and try to recall the words. Slowly they begin to float into your mind. Slowly you begin to remember and the song comes forth from your very own Soul.

Oh Great One who sees all and knows all
Can you please help me on this journey Home?
I have lost my way, please, can You see
And I beseech You to guide me back again

I have foundered many times on my journey outward
I look to you now for solace and comfort
You are my Beacon of Light that guides me back
To that special place where I was born

As clouds roll in off the distant horizon
And make their way over to this shore
I look upwards to you my dear one
For I am lost and without direction or hope

I know that I have missed you my Soul sublime
My highest Self gone aground inside of me
I look to you now to take me out of this place
Where my shattered dreams have come to fall

79

Now that You are near I feel free once again
Free from all those worries that terrified me in the past
I can see my way clear now and it leads back to You
My Self, my true Self, my Soul sublime

I welcome You and give thanks for You are with me again
And your place with me is so precious
I feel at home again, comfortable you know
Hopeful that this will be permanent and true

As I look out to sea and contemplate my future
Once again I realize that fate is at hand.
I must stay where I am and not run anymore
For only here in this moment can I be found and set free

So unpack all of my belongings
I will once again do as I've done in the past
But this time certain that I am bound to stay
For my life and purpose are here at last

I take refuge in the knowledge that You are near me
And I can call on You when I have need of Your grace
This is comforting to know
For so long now I've tried to do it all on my own

This has never worked as I wind up drained and tired
Sometimes the effort is too much to carry on
But with You at my side I feel hopeful and proud
I feel comfortable the whole day long

Thank you Soul dear for coming to my aid
Thank you for your presence and Love
Thank you for the lessons, the guidance and support
Thank you for seeing me through

I have a need to move along now as the tide wants to set in
I have a need to take advantage of its height
You are in my heart now, my awakening Soul
I feel happy; I feel joyful; I feel light

On this day of heartache and journeys to be taken
Where am I to go if not to my true Home?
For here is where I belong inside my very Self
To explore, to learn and to express what I am

This deepest part of me that knows no bounds
Sees no limitations, no fears, or worry
It reaches out to the world, to the light of "All That Is"
And rejoices in the essence of Its own sound.

This special chord that rings for only you, friend
Is your special gift of expression and light
This sound vibration from deep within your Soul
Is a gift to the world that is right

And now we say adieu to this experience in thought
Where our travels are gentle and sublime
We take into our hearts God's greatest gift, our Soul
With Its sweetness unto the end of time

As these words ring in your ear something stirs deep inside
A part of you that seldom lets Itself be known
But this song It knows and this song calls It forth
In response It rises upward, and then, takes you Home.

The Prince and The People

n a far off land lived a Prince of great importance. He ruled over a large number of people and, by all accounts, served them well. This Prince was the son of a great God who had sent him forth to work with His people. The Prince knew nothing of his Father's heavenly plan but agreed to act out his part in the affairs of His subjects.

When the Prince first arrived amongst the peoples of this principality, he took note of their attributes and inclinations. He noticed that the women, for example, were quite subdued and gave their authority to the men of the tribe. All the children listened only to the women, until a certain age, when the boys were then segregated and came under the rule of only the men. The men, he noticed, did not participate in the women's activities but isolated themselves and fraternized mainly with each other. They appeared to mingle with the women solely for the purposes of procreation.

One day the Prince decided he would challenge this state of affairs and proclaimed a decree that declared all women as equal to the men and that both groups should begin to interact with each other on a regular basis. The women of the tribe were delighted with this idea but the men were aghast. A delegation of men was sent to see the Prince to attempt to change his mind and to have the decree nullified. These men were deeply upset. They knew not why this decree had been issued but they believed that they could not tolerate it.

The Prince received this delegation of men graciously and spoke to them. "Gentlemen, I have no intent to harm you. I only wish to see you fraternize more with the women of the tribe and have them be considered equal to you in all ways."

"But, Sir," a spokesman shouted out, "it has never been this way. For many years now we have always delegated tribal responsibilities in such a fashion as to keep our two groups divided. This way we avoid conflict and difficulties with the other gender."

"But you know nothing of each other," the Prince replied. "How can you all live together and yet not know each other in the most fundamental sense?"

"We have no problem with that arrangement," the spokesman continued. "Our needs are simple and few. We procreate when necessary.

Otherwise, we remain separated. This way our varying and different needs never come into conflict. The women, we believe, receive what they need and we, in turn, remain with each other. It has worked this way for many years now and we are satisfied with this arrangement."

Just then a woman stepped forward as a representative from the women's delegation. They too had just arrived on the scene to discuss their concerns. "I do not agree with this gentleman at all," she stated. "The men claim that this system has worked for years but the fact is they are the only ones who seem happy with it. We, on the other hand, have been sad and lonely since this separation of the sexes took place eons ago. Contrary to what they claim our needs are not being met. We require more than mere procreation as a measure of contact. We require all sorts of stimulation - conversation, interaction, mingling, sharing, support and love. We desire all manner of such communication. But we have been relegated to our own separate camps for so long now that we know not how to approach each other. There are many women who feel this way and have said so to each other. But no one, from either group, has dared speak to the other for fear of upsetting that which has existed in the current fashion until now. We greet your decree with great joy, dear Prince, for we wish for more than what has been our lot thus far. We, for our part, wish for genuine interaction with these illustrious men."

At the Prince's request the two delegations withdrew to contemplate what had been shared. As usual, the women went to their own camp and the men did the same. Each group spoke of the matter well into the night. Such a topic had never before received so much attention. The men roared and bellowed their disapproval. The women shared their feelings and cried out their sadness, supporting each other in the process. The men continued their rampaging until their energy began draining away. The women paused in the midst of their discussion, with a promise of resuming later after they all had a proper rest. The men carried on till the wee hours of the morning. They could not, it seems, take any rest or delay the discussion without coming to a resolution. For them the issue was too threatening to let go even for a moment.

The next day the two delegations appeared before the Prince. Although he had not ordered them to work so diligently on the matter at hand, he was pleased nevertheless to see that both groups had taken the subject so seriously. The women's representative stepped forth first and declared once again their support for the decree as well as repeating their reasons. Then the spokesman for the men stepped forward and, much to everyone's surprise, also declared their support for the decree. The Prince, somewhat taken aback by this turnabout, asked the representative to explain this change of heart.

"You see Sir, it is like this," the spokesman began. "When we first addressed the question raised by the decree, we were all hurt and angry that you would make a declaration that was so contrary to our established ways. We bellowed and we shouted our disapproval throughout the night until we essentially exhausted ourselves. Then a strange thing happened. As we continued our discussion and listened to ourselves, we began to realize that we too were lonely and were missing this meaningful contact of which the women spoke. We began to realize that we also wanted more than we had thus far but were afraid to ask for it. As our discussion proceeded each of us in turn cited examples of lonely times beginning in childhood when we were first handed over to the elder men. Until that time we had enjoyed our contact with the adult women and the female children. We essentially saw no differences between us. But after the separation occurred, we were repeatedly schooled in the so-called differences until all we could see were these differences. By the time we reached adulthood we had forgotten what we once had in common with the females. Now as we listen to the adult women speak their truth we are once again aware of all our similarities, both those from childhood and those we appear to have today as adults. No one told us it would be so lonely to live separate lives cut off from each other. No one advised us that as time went on we would become ever more isolated and withdrawn until, as adults, we men would only rely on each other for sharing and comfort, and, as a result, other than for procreation, no further contact with the women would be maintained. We accept now that this is not satisfactory to us anymore. And we realize that we are the ones who have suffered the most because we cannot share anything meaningful with each other. The women, we notice, still can. They appear to be at ease with each other. We, on the other hand, are not. We tend to be reserved and unhappy much of the time. Therefore, we too wish for this change. So, at this time, Sir, we are respectfully willing to accept Your decree."

And a great sigh of relief was issued by all – the women, the men and the Prince. All, it seemed, were amply pleased with this outcome.

Shortly after that the Prince was reporting to his Father on the state of his principality.

"So, how did it go, My son?" the Father asked.

"Well, Father, you were quite right in predicting that this decree would elicit an interesting reaction. But I did not expect the men to come around so quickly. I am pleased, however, that they did."

"And so you should be, My son, for these people are quite resourceful and capable. After all, I have endowed them with My greatest virtues."

"But Father, why did you let them become separate in the first place?"

"Because they wanted that lesson, My son. They wanted to learn the value of true closeness so they chose the experience of separation first."

"I see," the Prince replied, "but why then have me issue the decree? Why not let them work it out for themselves?"

"Because every now and then these people need a reminder that I am about. They also want to be challenged so they can find their way back to their true Selves. They look for these challenges in their lives and they thrive on them. Left to their own devices they would find their way through these issues, but they prefer the excitement of a decree, as an example. In such a challenge they shine forth with their best efforts and quickly learn the lesson that might otherwise take eons. So with this decree I helped you accelerate the process. And such challenges are desirable at this point in their journey because I wish them to find their way Home more quickly for I am lonely and in need of their company."

With that said Father and Son embraced each other and the matter was left at that. As for the men and women of the tribe, they began to find their way toward each other again and they too learned to embrace and appreciate each other in new ways. As time moved on and other lessons were learned it soon could be said of them also:

That All Was Well in Their World

If you must know about your lot
Then ask a silly question
Don't hesitate to gather forth
That which creates a Nation

No one knows for sure of this
Or how we came to be here
But He doth know and He will show
What purpose for you be there

In your heart, the imprint wrote
Is of this life and purpose
Yours is there, ready to grow
When you set sights on surface

Then look inside from whence it came
And know you wrote it too
Because the signature at the end
Is not of one, but two!

Desert Island Meditation (I)

(Please record, or have someone read to you)

Imagine that you are on a desert island.

This is your home; this is your place to be.

You have chosen this location to distance yourself from the frantic activity of the world around you and about you.

You have chosen to relieve yourself of all these tensions and focuses and influences and demands upon your time and space.

You have chosen to come here to be with yourself, to be alone, to be centered.

In this place, in this place you can call an island, you are truly alone, alone with yourself in a manner that is not possible in the franticness of daily life and daily activity.

This island is symbolic of that inner core of your being, the center that represents your destiny and your purpose and your desire and your goal in this plane.

This island space is your refuge. You go there when you need to be with your Self, with your being, to recharge your Self, to reconnect your Self with the power of Spirit and Love. Here you can reaffirm to yourself the essence of your being, which comes from beyond you, comes from beyond this plane, comes from beyond this planet.

That essence presents itself to you in many different fashions, in many different ways, but within yourself it comes from the core of your being, the very center of your life.

As you access this part of yourself, you discover many things – that you are eternal – immortal – and universal, that you come from beyond time and space, that your power is infinite as is the power of God, that your wisdom is infinite as is the wisdom of the ages, that your essence is expansive and unlimited, that your access to knowledge and understanding is broad, beyond definition, beyond conventional experience.

In this realm at the center of your inner space, you are everything that you can conceive of: You are the ocean if you think of the ocean. You are the Earth if you think of the Earth. You are the stars and the planets if you think of those. You are these things, which is more than to say that you are simply aware of them. It is to say that you are inside these things, and they are inside you.

As your being thrusts out into the distant night, into the starlit sky, into the far reaches of the Universe, you experience all that you see before you.

You travel as a light body, able to merge with all you encounter, whether that is a planet, a star, a constellation, other entities, other universes. You are able to merge with all that you encounter because in that merging you experience these things.

From your island paradise you can reach out to "All That Is," you can expand into the Universe and absorb everything that exists there and bring it back within you. When you do this, you know that you are part of "All That Is." You know that for that brief moment you and the Father are One. You know that you can never be lost, a child of God can never be lost. You know that you exist beyond time and space, beyond your physical mortality, beyond all that defines you and all that limits you in your current existence. You exist forever.

Let yourself experience this now, this vastness of your capabilities, this expansiveness of your being, outward and into the beautiful night sky, into and around all the constellations of the Universe, into and around all Life forms that you recognize or imagine.

You are truly a child of the Universe and as such you are capable of all that you can imagine. The God Force places no limits upon you, exercises no constraints. As you expand your being from your island center and flower forth into all that surrounds you, you can grasp and absorb everything you encounter, everything represented by these external manifestations of the Life Force and of Being in disguise. This is a wonderful capability, brought to only those who are willing to see beyond their current limitations and their current definitions of Self.

This Self is forever and far-ever, expansive and capable beyond your wildest dreams.

Suppose that as you travel out into the Universe you are able to gather to yourself new wisdom, new knowledge, new experiences that enrich you and enlarge you, and bring them back with yourself, into your current existence, would you not indeed do so?

In this meditation that is what you can do, reach out far beyond your normal boundaries and embrace all Life, all experience, all wisdom that lies before you, that exists within the ethereal realms and is available to all who are willing to travel there. You can gather that all about you and bring it back with you, into your Self, into your Center and let it germinate and grow within you, and use it in your current life. This you can do, and perhaps surprise yourself in the process.

The wisdom of the ages is available to all. Expansiveness beyond current boundaries is available to all.

Allow yourself now to return to the center of yourself, to your island paradise from where you left on this journey.

Imagine you are sitting in the sand on the shore of your island – cross legged, eyes closed, warm sun above, birds overhead, wind blowing, waves splashing on the shore. You are now grounded in your Self, centered in your Being, and all that you ventured forth to see and to experience is with you now. You have brought it back with you.

See your center expanded and grown larger as a result of this journey.

See your Self larger than before, wiser than before, richer than before.

Allow yourself to rest – within this space – as long as you need – and when you are ready return to that place from whence you left on this journey. Return to that place with all of these gifts. Know that you are blessed. Know that you are loved. And know that you are wealthy beyond belief. The God Force wishes you to know this, wishes you to have this.

It is yours to have, and to hold, and to maintain, and – to keep forever. Know this:

And All Will Be Well in Your World

91

Desert Island Meditation (II)

(Please record, or have someone read to you)

Imagine once again that you are on a desert island. Imagine the sound of the surf – birds flying overhead – wind in the trees – sunshine all around – a warm summer day. The air is dry. It's a day filled with promise and possibility.

You are not alone this time. There are many all around you, many whom you do not recognize because their appearance is unfamiliar to you. These are friends of yours, however, friends from another time and another place, who have come to join you in your peacefulness and your solitude. They have come to remind you of who you are and why you came here to this planet. They have come to instruct you in all manner of things important to your purposes in this realm.

You allow them to come closer. You look at their appearance, their shape. It is kind of fuzzy and hazy, not clear to you who they are or even what they are. But you do experience a sense of recognition, a sense of familiarity. These entities, these individuals, gather around you, sit with you, on your beach, in the beautiful, bright sunlight of the day.

You begin to notice that they are speaking to you, sharing with you important information, familiar information, but alien at the same time. It feels like a family has gathered, a family from a distant plane, from a distant place, a family that you sense you may belong to but you're not quite sure. The recognition is not fully available as of yet.

You listen and you notice. They speak to you in an unfamiliar tongue, yet it sounds familiar. They convey, through feeling and gesture, the essence of their message, the essence of their purpose, and the essence of your purpose in turn. Just allow this to occur. Allow yourself to absorb whatever information they are sharing with you. These are your friends and you are safe. All they wish for now is to remind you of who you are.

You are one of them, they tell you. You have come to this place from a far-off land, far-off in the sense of another galaxy, another place, another time. And you have come here to participate in a process that they want you to understand is very important. As a participant you are to be a contributor and a facilitator of that process, as are many others like you. They remind you of your purpose, of your part in this process. They remind you of how important this work is. They remind you again and again who you are, a child of the All Powerful, a child of All-That-Is, a child of the Power of Love.

You really are not alone and you never have been, they tell you. You have always been in the company, in the very good company, of friends and family. Not so visible to you in this realm, they point out, but present nevertheless, as present as everything else around you that you can see, feel and touch. Their presence is of a spiritual form, a pure energy, a grand energy, a spirit that surrounds, fills, embraces and touches. They've been whispering to you for ages, for as long as you've been here this time, sharing with you knowledge, secrets, insights and intuitions, into the purpose of all this, into the purpose of this life and your place in it.

The Light and Love of God are with you, they remind you. You are perfect. You are a being of Light come from the past and the future to present to the world gifts that have been provided you by the Power of Love, the Power of Creation. Creation insists that these gifts be shared, as it does of all with whom It provides such favors. The Power of Creation provides such gifts to ensure that Its blessings are passed on. Gifts are not meant to be hoarded but to be shared. And your gifts are to be shared in equal measure amongst those who come in contact with you and in whom you recognize a need to help and to guide.

This same guidance is being provided to you, you realize, by those who are sitting with you in this circle on this beautiful sunny day. They are your friends from beyond, from the nether regions, from the future, from the past, from the present, all gathered to confer with you and to bless you with their love, affection, and intention.

"Go out and spread the word, my son, my daughter, this is your task."

"Help those in distress."

"Love everyone."

"Share your wealth."

"Share your gifts and your love."

"Spread happiness."

"Spread joy."

"Encourage beauty and wonder."

"Encourage love and self-empowerment."

"Encourage self-expression to the highest – in the most high."

"Do this, and all will be blessed, all will grow, all will reach out toward the heavens, toward that from whence they came."

"And know that they are blessed. And know that they are safe. And know that the Love of God is with them all the time."

"This is your message."

"This is your gift."

"This is your purpose as a speaker, as a sharer of the truth."

"The Lord High God has no other requirements than for you to share that which He has given you. And that which you give in turn is to be shared as well by those who receive it."

And then they remind you that, as this process unfolds, the beauty and lushness of nature and life are passed on to spread themselves through the entire race of man. And, in so doing, the race is cleansed and purified and rendered "holy" in His eyes, as it was created, as it was intended to be. This creativity and cleansing are highly important as part of a vast cleansing process that includes the entire community of man and the entire planet. Every being, every entity, every creature, every life form requires this cleansing at this time, and it is through "man" that the cleansing is to be provided. It is through the cleansing of "man" that the entire planet is to be cleansed, and that the Word of God will be brought forth to fruition.

See yourself as part of this process. See yourself as part of this ever-unfolding pattern of enlightenment and growth. You will be received. You will be understood and welcomed. All that you have to offer will be understood and accepted. You have nothing to fear. The Lord High God is with you all the time. All your needs are met. All is well in your world. You are safe. You are loved. You are greatly appreciated and you are always welcome in the House of the High Ones of your Inner Circle.

As your Circle breaks up and your Friends depart, as they wander off in various directions, you are aware that you are wiser, that you have received something precious, that you have been imbued with feelings of creativity and power that you did not enjoy before. You are stronger and more alive, more willing and more faithful to the purposes and causes that brought you here in the first place. You are richer now and, as such, you have more to offer. Each expansion of your growth means you have more to contribute. There is no end to this process. It only continues to expand, and within it, you continue to expand as well. As you stand up on your beautiful sandy beach and look around you, you notice that everything feels cleaner, brighter, crisper, even more beautiful than it did before.

95

It already was so beautiful, but now, is even more so. And you within it are equally more beautiful, more clean, more pristine, more powerful than you've ever imagined or felt.

With this in mind, in hand and in heart, you go forth on your mission of mercy, on your mission of caring and of sharing. You are the one who came to do this. You are the one who has so much to offer. It is up to you now to share what you know and to invite those who are interested to share what they know with you. The Light and Love of God are with you always. You are blessed. Know this is so. Know that you are safe. Know that all your needs are met.

And Know That All Is Well in Your World

96

We bring you news of far off lands
Of places beyond the rainbows
To share with you our future plans
That have you part of this show

Brilliant colors, lovely hues
All arranged in sequence
Part of this great tapestry
You call life and regence

Never let your colors dull
Or falter in your winning
'Cause you'll know there's no chance
Of returning to beginning

What you shine you carry forth
Into the next event
All cued up, ready to go
Just waiting for your offense

Push it out, let it roar
Hold back not, no longer
Let it out this suppressed lore
And shine out every color

The Traveller

here once was a man who came to Earth because he wanted to learn some important lessons. He had travelled far and wide throughout his time experiencing many different forms of existence. He had travelled as a spirit in other planes, spheres and galaxies. He had spent some time as a guardian of comets and planets in various constellations of stars. Our young man was tired of these challenges and now wanted to experience something different. So he asked the Creator if he could come to Earth to try this experience for a time and his wish was granted.

Upon his arrival on the Earth plane our young man discovered many important facts about himself. The first thing he realized was that now he had a body, a dense body composed of the same matter that supported all life on Earth. He also discovered that he had a Heart which was designed to guide him forth on his earthly adventure. In his other planes of experience he never had such an instrument and, therefore, had to rely on other faculties to guide him along. This Heart was a curious instrument which he set about to understand. It was not at all like the heart that beat in his chest, but rather was more of a "feeling nature" that advised him of his every circumstance and his experience within it. He could experience pain as never before. He could experience joy that made him soar. He could experience ecstasy and disappointment all in the same moment. A truly amazing instrument this "heart nature" was.

With his Heart as his guide our young man set forth on his journey through Earth life. He knew he was here to accomplish something important but that this would only be revealed as he went along his path. Part of the journey, he realized, was discovery – that there was to be an element of surprise in all his experiences so that their impact would be maximized. As he proceeded on his journey, he encountered other individuals with similar bodies to his and he looked for who they were in their Hearts. With some, he could see a faint glimmer in their Hearts, but with many more he could barely see anything at all. This was truly puzzling for he envisioned himself as like all the creatures around him and fully expected to see in them what he now recognized in himself.

His confusion became so great that our young man called upon the Creator to help him understand these bewildering circumstances. And the Creator came to speak with him in his Heart.

"My son, you have come to planet Earth to learn many things. With your Heart as your guide you can clearly hear My voice and proceed without difficulty on your journey. With such an open capacity to receive you fully expected to meet others like yourself. But what you have found are many individuals closed off from their source which is Me."

"But Lord, why is this so? Why are we not all alike?" he asked with some alarm in his voice.

"But you are, My son, all very much alike. What you have encountered here are individuals who have become closed off from their inner Self. And so they appear lost to you as you cannot clearly see the spark from their Heart which you would then recognize as very much like your own."

"But what am I to do, Lord? What am I to say? I cannot be here if I am to feel so alone. That pain is unbearable to me."

"I know," the Creator replied. "I did not send you here to be lonely. I wish for you to rejoice in this experience called Life. We must do something to remedy this situation. I will consult with my angels and return to you shortly with an answer."

While waiting to hear again from the Creator our young man continued his journey and came upon a beautiful woman with a Heart all aglow. "How wonderful," he said to himself. "Someone to whom I can relate and perhaps share this experience."

"Greetings my lady, would you please help me? I am here on a journey of discovery and growth and I am uncertain as to how to proceed. Can you offer me any suggestions?"

"Well," said the lady, "I can certainly try. First, you must determine why you are here. Is it your task to simply wander about and experience the Earth as it appears to you? Or is it perhaps your task to influence Life here in some positive or growth-fulfilling fashion?"

"I am sorry, I do not know what you mean," he replied. "I arrived here with my Heart open and fully expected to meet others like myself. It had been my task in the past to merely look after the environment to which I was assigned. I assumed that this might be my task once again."

"Very well," replied the woman, "I believe I can see your dilemma. In the past you were used to caretaking and maintaining, but not influencing, in order to promote positive-oriented growth."

"What do you mean?" he asked again.

"Well, in caretaking one's task is to simply maintain a situation as it is, perhaps to influence on occasion to a slight degree, but essentially just to maintain. On planet Earth we are all involved in a growth experiment and that requires some effort on our parts."

"On our parts?" he repeated.

"Yes," she went on, "on all our parts. There are many like myself who have their Hearts fully opened and our task is to help those whose Hearts have not yet opened."

"You mean those individuals whom I saw earlier with barely a glimmer had Hearts that were simply closed?"

"That is correct," she replied, "and it is these individuals whom we are here to help."

"I see then," he repeated. "So that would be my task, too, I presume, since I have come here with my Heart fully opened."

"Likely so," she replied, "although the Creator could tell you for certain."

Just then the Creator returned and addressed our young man from within his Heart. "I see you have already found your answer."

"Yes, Lord, I believe I have. I am here to influence this Life in the most positive way that I can and help those individuals whose hearts are closed. I will go forth now and complete this task as I believe I have been assigned to do. Thank you, Lord, for returning to me with an answer so quickly."

"Oh, and how did I do that?" the Creator asked.

"By sending me that beautiful angel in the form of a woman to explain to me my purpose, and to show it by her example."

"I see you are learning quickly, My son. I hope all your future questions can be answered so easily. I will return to you again at another time."

And our young man proceeded on his journey, helping light the lights of those in the darkness and spreading good humor and openness wherever he went. And from that time on, with the Creator at his side, a sense of his purpose in view and a Heart fully opened, he knew:

That All Would Be Well in His World

An Ocean Voyage

Guided Meditation
(Record, or have someone read to you)

Imagine you are on an ocean voyage. The seas are calm. The sky is beautiful, not a cloud anywhere. Only a few mists of white gently drifting with the breeze. Yours is a small craft, very small, which carries you across the seas to visit various worlds that have remained, for the most part, uninhabited and unexplored.

On the first of your island stops you encounter a strange individual. Very tall you would say, a giant even, who lives alone on this tiny island that you have set ashore on. The giant greets you and receives you with great warmth. He asks you to join him for a time and proceeds to tell you a story about yourself, a story he could not possibly know unless he knew you or could see inside of you.

The story goes that when you were a child and were first set loose upon this world various actions were put into place to protect you and guide you forth. Although it appeared you were alone at first, this truly never was the case. Into your small craft went amulets and jewels and other precious items all designed to take you further on your journey through life. Some of these items were for immediate use and others were for later on. Some items had magical powers that you could activate when needed.

"One day," he goes on, "when you were sailing about the world in your tiny craft, you dropped one of your amulets over the side and into the water it went. A fish swimming by scooped it up and swallowed it whole. This fish was in turn caught by a fisherman who, when preparing it for dinner, threw out the amulet as so much unnecessary waste. The amulet was then found by a child who took it to her mother who exchanged it for a large loaf of bread. From there, the amulet travelled further until it found itself in a Castle with other forms of treasure to be traded for more valuable items. Eventually the amulet found its way to a market where it was purchased by a sea trader who greatly admired its beauty. So, from your hand to the sea, through several more hands, your amulet has circumnavigated the globe. Now here you are talking to me, a giant of a man who lives alone on an island by the sea. So what is the point of this story you may ask?"

And the giant carries on with his task of explaining your presence now at his island home.

"Now that the amulet is so well travelled, where would it likely be at this time?"

"With you sir?" you then ask.

"Why yes," he replies, "with me."

And with that said the giant reaches into his pocket and hands you the amulet. "But how did you know it was for me?" you ask.

"Because you showed up here and what other reason would you have to be here than to collect your amulet."

"You mean I knew why I was coming here all along?"

"Yes," he answers, "in a fashion, in that your sense of direction brought you to a place where you needed to be if only to retrieve something you had lost. We always return for the things we have lost or misplaced."

With that said, the giant man retreats from the scene and returns to the interior of the island from where he had come. With the amulet in hand you return to your vessel and proceed again out to sea. "Very strange," you say to yourself, "I did not even know that the amulet was gone. And here by good fortune it is returned to me. How truly wonderful this is. I wonder what awaits me next."

A storm then rises shortly after you set out and tosses your small vessel about. "I cannot steer," you say to yourself, "so I must let go and allow the vessel its own free rein." You then nod off to sleep while the storm rages all about you. Early the next day you awaken to find yourself lying in the sand on another island shore where no one seems to dwell. Some birds land nearby to hunt for food and a few turtles scurry along the sand heading back to the sea. You sit up, dust yourself off and locate your craft which is higher up on the shore. You proceed to look about this new domain to familiarize yourself with the area. Just then a man in a majestic white robe appears on the scene. You notice that he has a long white beard and is carrying a wooden staff. He greets you with a curious look and speaks to you.

"What are you doing here?"

"I don't know," you reply. "A storm overtook me in my small vessel last night and I surrendered to its might. This morning I find myself here on this island and I am not sure where I am."

"Follow me," the bearded man continues. "I know why you came. You are here to receive instruction which I am to provide. This is to help you on your journeys across the sea."

So up a hill you go, trailing behind the bearded man, wondering what adventure lies ahead. At the top of the hill you come upon a beautiful garden with a structure of columns, arranged in a circle at its center and highest point. The bearded man directs you to sit within the columns and prepare yourself to receive wisdom from the Creator. As you sit, you notice a small pebble in the sand which you reach for and hold. The man notices this and says to you. "That is good as your instruction will now surely take hold." Shortly after that he awakens you, for it appears you fell asleep and did not notice what was going on while you were receiving your instruction. But he assures you that you have indeed received much wisdom this day and, because of the stone in your hand, it will surely take hold.

Your instruction done, the wise old man returns you to the beach so that you can set out once again upon the sea. In your hand is your stone which you have retrieved and which you feel a need to carry with you from now on. You are not so sure about its place in your life but decide to place it amongst the other jewels and gifts that have been with you since you began your journey. The amulet is there, as are other artifacts that have had a place in your history. This stone is the latest addition you realize and part of a continuum of gifts that the Universe has provided to you. Realizing this, you feel blessed once again, knowing you are looked after, knowing that wherever you go your needs will be met.

It is another sunny day and a breeze is blowing lightly across your craft's bow. Ahead is another island that beckons you forth. This time you are certain that you will go ashore here as you now know that you must follow your heart. As you arrive you are greeted by a group of friendly faces. You notice that there is something strangely familiar about these people as they help you come ashore. They greet you warmly, ask you how you are, and ask you about your travels. You tell them of your meeting with the Giant and your meeting with the wise old man. You tell them the story of the amulet as it was related to you and you tell them the story of the garden and the columns where you received instruction.

"And what do you remember of your instruction?" they ask.
"Well, nothing really," you answer, "except that when I sighted this island I knew I had to land here."
"How is that?" they ask again.
"I don't know for sure," you reply, "except that the feeling inside was so strong that I just had to follow my heart and land here. Strangely enough that was not the case with the first or second islands I visited. At the first island I just came upon it and went ashore to look around and

explore. Here I met the giant who told me the story of the amulet and then returned it to me. At the second island I was blown ashore by that fierce storm that overtook me. There I met the wise old man who took me into the garden for instruction and then returned me to the sea. Upon sighting this third island I deliberately chose to land. I felt drawn here and then compelled to come ashore."

"So you knew you belonged here?" asked one of the members of the group. "Well yes," you reply, "this island felt vaguely familiar, something like Home perhaps."

"And that is so," another voice echoed. "When we set out on our respective journeys, we know not what we are to encounter but bit by bit pieces are given to us that help us find a direction. Eventually that direction becomes ever more clear and we know then where it is we want to go. When we choose Home, we choose consciously that place that we recognize from within as our place of origin. We may never be absolutely certain, but certain enough to choose that final leg in the journey and return ourselves to where we began. Once there, we realize that it is different now as we have travelled far and learned much, but it remains familiar all the same. For how would we know for certain if it were not for that feeling that began stirring so strongly within as we came closer and closer."

"I understand," you say to them. "This has been an adventure, a dream perhaps, a dream of lost loves and retrieved gifts, a dream of wisdom and danger, of beginnings and endings and all things in between. My journey is my very own and therefore mine to keep. And now that I am Home, I know that I will never be alone again."

"And you were never really alone," they continue. "We were there with you all along, sometimes in spirit, sometimes in form. You see, one of us was the Giant that you first heard inside, and another was the stone. One of us was the amulet which you early had thrown. One of us was the wise man and one of us the sea, some of us the birds above, some of us the breeze. All of us were present," they go on, "to help you find your way. You were never alone really because we were there to help guide you Home."

And the entire group was happy and joyful as all proceeded to return to their respective homes on the island. And you too follow along, winding your way up a now familiar path and discover for yourself that you are now Home as well.

And All Is Well in Your World

Stranger things have happened you say, than merely being found on this plane, searching about for a meaning or tune, something to guide one around. Where did it come from this purpose of ours that sees us chasing about, looking for love in all the wrong places, drinking from empty cups? The Earth is upon us like a great grey whale sweeping across the ocean in search of its next meal. The Earth is our Mother and giver of life, expressing our longing for Him who sent us down here on this two-week vacation from stardust cleansing and comet chasing. "Have a break" He said that day. "Try a little Earth time. Send me a postcard, don't forget to write, or, at least, come back happy."

The Wrong Body

his is a story about a man who found himself trapped inside a body. That is, through some misfortune of circumstances, he found he was locked in a body and a situation that he had not intentionally chosen. How did this happen and why a "wrong" body? These are interesting questions indeed. Let us look in on the scene to see what actually happened.

You must first be willing to consider the proposition that a person chooses their body before entering the Earth Plane. At what point does this choosing take place? Moments before birth on some occasions and, at other times, much earlier in the gestation cycle. Now our man David was typically given to dawdling, so his choice, as expected, was made at the last possible moment before birth. Prior to that he had been occupied with other interests that kept him busy and out of touch with his impending incarnation. Remember, this man chose the wrong body, so to speak. How this happened is the subject of our story. So –

Once there was a man named David who sought to reincarnate into the world of matter. David was not known for his attentiveness in matters relating to the flesh or his upcoming occupancy there. David preferred distraction overall, anything to keep him from worrying about his future. You see there was a time when all he did was worry. Worry about this, worry about that, worry about everything he could imagine and more.

There came a day when David could no longer tolerate worrying. So he decided to stop it altogether and to occupy himself with as much trivia as he could. In this effort David became quite successful. He was able to master the art of mind trickery in which he kept himself busy with one set of thoughts in order to avoid another set, namely worries. David became so good at this strategy that he eventually forgot about his worrying and became totally enmeshed in his new method of avoidance. He succeeded to such an extent that he even forgot to attend to the simplest of basic needs regarding himself and his life in general.

Now the Masters of the Universe were hard at work trying to find David a suitable situation and body in which to incarnate. This situation would have to be tailored to his current needs to learn certain lessons. As They toiled over Their task, scratching Their heads, David remained distracted in his usual way, totally oblivious to the huge efforts that were being made for him. As he continued his pattern of distraction and dawdling, a thought came to one of the Members of the Team to install David in a "wrong body." Now, what did this mean, actually? How could you in fact put someone in a wrong body, for no matter where you were placed, it would have to be right for the lessons you were about to learn? Now David did have his list of lessons to address, but he remained oblivious to these as he went about his various distractions and busy work. The Masters decided to go ahead with Their plan. They would find the exact wrong body for David and install him there. Then They would watch to see what happened.

As David was occupying himself with one of his many diversions, the call came that it was time to incarnate. "Please be prepared to incarnate, sir, as we have only a few moments before birth takes place," the announcement was made. David lifted his head long enough to try to notice what was happening and then 'swoosh' there he was exiting the birth canal of his new mother. Before he could fully realize what had happened, he had been swathed in linens and placed in his new mother's arms. The birthing had taken place.

David's new mother, it turns out, was a very large gorilla who had lived in captivity since her birth. She was so used to humans that she thought herself to be human as well and behaved much as they did, mimicking their every gesture and mode of conduct. Over the years she had acquired a vast array of human abilities and was certainly quite comfortable in their environment. The fact that she now had a new human baby was no surprise to her and seemed quite natural indeed. Natalie, our gorilla mother, was highly pleased with her new son whom she promptly named David for some unexplainable reason. Perhaps it was because this name

was the most common in her environment and, therefore, spoken most easily. At any rate David, the new son, looked up at his mother in total surprise and began to wonder what was happening. The last thing he had heard was the call to prepare for incarnation and now here he was in the hands of this gorilla mother. "What has happened," he asked himself rather anxiously?

As it was, David's memory was still intact from prior to this incarnation, even though he was now a tiny baby again on the Earth Plane. As a result he knew he could contact his Higher Self and ask for direction in this most unusual of circumstances. After all, there had to be an error, and he strongly wanted to be on his way into an appropriate human lifetime.

Meanwhile Natalie, our gorilla mother, was enjoying her new son and displayed him to everyone who visited them. The neighboring gorillas came by to see as did the human caretakers of this home for captive creatures. All were somewhat astonished as to this baby's appearance but, for some strange reason, no one really questioned what they saw in front of them.

David, however, was now frantic for answers. For how could this be that he was born to a mother gorilla? Just as he was pondering this question yet another time in his mind, his High Self did respond to his frantic queries, "Well, my dear fellow, I see you are in quite a mess here. You thought you were being delivered to a human family but here you are with a gorilla mother. How very puzzling, indeed!"

"Yes, High Self, I am most puzzled," David replied. "How did this happen to me? What can I do?"

"Well, my dear fellow," his High Self continued, "as it turned out, prior to this incarnation, you were once again preoccupied and distracted as has been your pattern lately and so the Masters of the Universe decided to play a joke on you. They decided to give you to a gorilla mother to awaken you from your usual pattern of disconnectedness and inattentiveness. Once the point was made, and after having learned an important lesson, you were then to be reassigned to a proper human family. Now We can see that this has happened. You have awakened to the fact that you are here with this gorilla mother and you can also see that she has become quite attached to you. You now appear to be quite attentive. So now we must ask ourselves if this situation can be altered or remedied. Do we reverse the process and return you to the world of spirit or do we leave you here to be raised as a gorilla?" he said with a slight chuckle.

"But High Self," David pleaded, "should I not be with a human family?" "Yes, of course," was the reply, "but you do have a human body that was somehow issued from this creature."

"But High Self," David continued, "is that possible under the laws of nature?"

"You are quite right," his High Self replied barely able to contain Himself, "but then again here you are, are you not, a human baby born from a gorilla mother?"

"I understand the mistake, High Self," David quickly replied. "But what do I do now?"

And his High Self, calmer now, replied, "I'll have to confer with the Masters of the Universe and return to you shortly."

And with that David was left to wait for an answer to his dilemma. Meanwhile the Masters were busy hatching another plan to have him removed to a more appropriate family, a human family of course. It seems that the original debate about where to place David had not really been settled when, as his birth was about to take place, They too had been momentarily distracted. Their joking about "wouldn't be interesting if We gave him to a gorilla instead of directing him to a more suitable human mother" had been realized. So before They could fully appreciate the impact of such a move They had inadvertently sent him to Natalie. "And somewhere," one of Them speculated with some dismay, "might there be a human family with a baby gorilla?" The discussion was going on with some animation when David's High Self came to call upon Them. They then proceeded to explain all, pointing out that in Their distractedness, They too had succumbed to inattentiveness and now this mess was at hand. They asked that David be informed of this while the necessary steps could be undertaken to correct the situation.

So now, a cosmic dilemma was at hand. It seemed that two babies were possibly in the wrong hands and, therefore, two "families" would need to be restored. As it turns out, David's human family was still awaiting him so the second part of the mistake had not occurred, much to the relief of all concerned. All that was required then was the proper delivery of a baby gorilla to Natalie, in concert with the transfer of David to his appropriate human family, once birth there was imminent. As soon as this was clarified, the Masters set about making the necessary corrections. While she slept, Natalie's human baby was quietly substituted with a more appropriate gorilla baby and David was momentarily returned to spirit to await his upcoming incarnation.

Interestingly enough, after David arrived back on the Spirit Plane he paid close attention to every detail of the preparations for his impending incarnation. He oversaw the Masters' plan to have him introduced to a proper human family and he noted carefully all the characteristics of the birth parents and the lessons he was to learn. When birth finally did occur, it was observed by all present that baby David was very attentive to his surroundings and that he responded very well to all forms of stimuli. Some even thought this to be rather exceptional for a newborn. "This baby," all agreed, "is extremely alert." "Such a pleasure," the parents reflected, "for this child will indeed be a joy to rear." For his part, David had now forgotten who he was and why he was here. In his world now, all was a symphony of color and sound, taste and smell, and all types of sensory experiences. It was clear, however, even at this early point in his new life, that he was eager to experience it all.

And All Was Well in His World

Let Your Feelings Be Your Guide

The Light of all eternity shines with me now
My feelings light up my life and show me who I am
How I find my way is determined by them
They light up my path and show me the way

When I was young oh how I felt so many things
Then came the day when no longer could I stand the pain
My world was chaos then, filled with sorrow and grief
So I closed up to protect that fragile Self within

Years would go by before I could reopen myself again
I was forced to by circumstances beyond me, or so it seemed
Life dealt me blows which I later recognized as my own
To awaken me to that sorrow deep within my Soul

I've worked hard to find my way back to the Light
To that place where within me I could feel once again
There my Heart shone forth into my face
And shed light on all that I had concealed

Now I see how I closed my tender-hearted Self
How I froze in the face of destiny
My troubles swirled around me like a constant source of grief
And I fell to sleep out of fear

I am awakening now, so I'm told, to the deep sleep within
Where I've stored all my troubles and pain
I fight my way through to that center once again
Where I can come forth and be true

My life moves forward as of this day
When I committed to do this work of finding my true Self within
I have engaged all manner of demons on this, my journey
To return to my Source deep inside

I wish for life to fill me now, to bring me all that it can
I am thirsty for experience and for growth
I want lavish riches in my Soul to fill me so plain
So that I can enjoy all that I behold

This work is difficult as I've imagined and thus learned
But no more so than any task requiring Love
This journey embellishes me with its purpose
And fills me with Life and with Soul

That is my gift to myself, my own holy Soul
To have, to hold and to behold
This Heart of mine that bled before is now healed of its wounds
And can enjoy all that Life brings it forth

Let there never be a return to the old where hurts cramp me up
And fill me with bitterness and pain
I am awake now it seems so I can move ahead
And enjoy all that Life has assigned

Oh glory to you my sweet Soul for coming to me this day
I thank you from the bottom of my Heart
We too can sing together now the praises of Love
That take us forward on this journey through time

Never let it be said that one so deserving
Could not find his way Home
All that are to follow will see this Light in turn
And know that their journey can be won

I take you with me now my sweet Soul
For you are here in my hands
And together we can be so bold

"Move on," you say to me, "move on, my son
The Light wishes for us to do so"

My Heart fills with joy and Love
Knowing all along you are my Soul
My feelings tell me you are there and always have been thus
Till the sleep came over me once before

By awakening to Your touch do I know who You are
And can find my own truth in Your eyes
You show me Dear Love what my purpose is to be
By Your inspired and attentive design

I am pleased we are here together, my dear
I am pleased that our love is so strong
For how could I find you my Soul sublime
If you did not call me from deep in my Heart

I have your answer dear and know this to be true
That you and I are forever to be born
In this life, or another, we join with each other

And we Soar, And we Soar . . . And we Soar

The Magic Lamp

nce upon a time there was a fair maiden named Genevieve. We have seen her before in other stories and now she returns to us in this new tale. Genie is an eternal Soul who appears periodically to advise us on circumstances that may be beyond our control, circumstances which can lead us away from ourselves and back once again as we are invited to determine the key to our individual dilemmas.

On this particular day Genie was walking about her garden and came upon a lamp. She raised the lamp up to examine it and exclaimed, "Oh, what a beautiful lamp. What magic do you hold for me, dear lamp? For now that I have you in my possession you must respond to my wishes. And I wish to be taken out of myself and transported to another realm where I can learn to appreciate my life more fully." The lamp acknowledged her request by twinkling like a bright ray of sunlight and soon Genie was swept away from her garden and taken to a land of strange and beautiful sights. As requested, the lamp transported her to a place totally alien and unfamiliar to her usual context of life.

When Genie arrived in this strange new place, she was confronted by a contingent of ghoulish creatures who accosted her in a most brazen and aggressive manner. These were short, dark, stout creatures with pointed ears and large sunken eyes. Their appearance was most disturbing.

"Who are you?" they asked. "What do you want? You do not belong here. Why are you here?" they continued, pressing Genie for answers.

"Well you see," Genie replied, "I was walking in my garden when I came upon this lamp." She then held it up for all to see. "I asked the lamp to take me out of myself so that I could gain a new perspective on my life. And that is how I arrived here."

"I see," they replied in unison. "Well then, welcome to our land. Can we be of assistance to you in any way?"

"Why, yes," replied Genie. "I have need of your help to find my way about in this land. For I have lessons to learn and much to appreciate before I am returned to my regular life."

One of the ghouls stepped forward, announced himself as head of the band, and took her by the hand. Genie allowed herself to be led away. The whole contingent followed and off they all went into this mysterious and beautiful place.

While walking along strange things began to happen. Flowers would peek up out of the ground to look at her and then retreat in apparent shyness. Trees bowed to have a closer look as she walked by. Streams grew quieter and the winds softened when her presence was near. Animals scurried by and stopped to look her over. Wherever she went, she was greeted with curiosity and surprise, yet none of the creatures spoke to her or approached her. They all hid or retreated as she passed by them.

Genie became uncomfortable with the reactions from the creatures and the vegetation around her. She asked the head ghoul why this situation existed? Why was she a witness to such behavior from the animals and the plants? "Well," he said, "whenever visitors come to our land we escort them through this area to see how they will react to our environment. We also wish to see how our environment reacts to them. In typical fashion, the inhabitants of our environment retreated from you as you appear strange and, of course, unfamiliar to us all. But do not be fooled. This does not mean that you are unwanted or unappreciated. It simply means that you are strange to us."

Genie was puzzled by this explanation. In her homeland she was used to being greeted and welcomed wherever she went and never did she experience this type of shyness or withdrawal in her presence. This was a totally new experience for her and she was unsure how to respond. As the procession continued, she noticed more strange things happening. Creatures, large and small, were beginning to follow her and the accompanying ghouls. She had not noticed this before as that group had been far behind, but now she could plainly see that a large number of followers had assembled and more were joining in as the procession carried on.

Genie's discomfort continued to grow. Finally, in anger, she turned to face this gathering multitude.
"Why are you all following me?" she shouted. "I have come here to learn about myself and all of you are staring at me as if I am some kind of oddity. Why do you do this?"
The creatures looked around at each other feeling puzzled themselves now.
"Why is this woman yelling at us?" some asked. "We are not harming her or threatening her in any way. We just wish to see, to have the opportunity to know her."
The head ghoul stopped the procession to address the matter. "My dear madam," he began, "you are a guest among us. As such it is not appropriate that you question us. Rather, we are permitted to question

you. As you are in our company and are now travelling across our land, these creatures are understandably curious as to whom you are and your purpose here. But please note, no one is attacking you and no one is impeding your progress. They are all simply observing you."

"But I find it so distressing," Genie stated, "to have all of these creatures following me and staring at me. I am not at all used to this. I am certainly not used to being observed so closely."

"But madam," the head ghoul continued, "did you not ask to be taken outside of yourself? Did you not ask to learn more about yourself from a totally different perspective?"

"Why yes I did," she conceded. "Is that what is happening here? Am I being examined by you and this large group of creatures so that I can learn more about myself?"

"Well yes, in a way, that is true," was the reply. "All these eyes are upon you and the normal pace of life here has slowed while you pass through our domain. This allows more of us to look into you and later report our observations. You see, these eyes are really only extensions of your imagination and we are all simply different parts of you looking back at your life. We are the externalization of your wish to examine yourself, and you find that most uncomfortable, do you not?"

"Why yes," Genie answered, "I do. So these creatures that I see here are not really looking at me. It is I, through their manifestation, who is looking at myself."

"That is correct," the head ghoul answered.

"But then, sir ghoul, are you not also part of this process? Are you not in turn another extension of my imagination?"

"Yes of course," the head ghoul replied. "I am that part of you that commands this process and helps you in achieving your goal. I am your 'commander in chief', your actualiser of hidden potentials. You come to me when you want important work done. And I, in turn, appear to you in a guise most suitable to your request."

"So where am I really?" Genie then asked.

"You are within yourself," the ghoul replied.

And then all about her disappeared in a flash. Genie was once again standing in her garden looking around for the lamp she had discovered earlier. There it was, lying at her feet, still twinkling in the sunlight, still inviting her to pick it up and take another journey.

"You are a very clever lamp," she thought to herself. "I wonder if you are not also a part of me? Did I dream you into existence or are you really there at my feet, beckoning me forward?"

With that thought Genie left the garden to return to her castle home. Along the way, she noticed that the plants and the creatures about her appeared to be different, but yet similar somehow to the ones from the dream. The creatures and plants, for their part, went about their business as usual, not noticing whether Genie was there or not, and not at all concerned about her presence in the garden. They seemed to know that she was no threat to them, and they, none to her.

"How sweet," she thought. "This is how I am used to my life, but now it seems even more special. I must have learned something new on my dream journey for I don't believe I noticed before how beautiful this all is, how very still and how very precious." "I must journey more often," she continued, "for a journey away from myself brings me back more enlightened and more aware than before I went. Now I can see things I didn't notice previously. And I do not in the least feel self-conscious about it. This is simply an amazing life, isn't it?"

And with that thought in her heart she went merrily on her way to enjoy yet another wonderful day.

And All Was Well in Her World

Children play so hard and fast
They make no rules, their play to last
Beyond the limits we would impose
With well chose words, but not in prose

For we would not adventure dare
And break the rules we oft prepare
To help us stay in safety's lair
Lest we fall prey to our despair

But children say "Oh no we can't
Find our way in this old chant
Give us the new and then prepare
To give way please, and let us dare"

A Shared Journey

here once was a man named Maury who had left his home to travel about the world in a small vessel. Maury had been to many places and experienced many things. His last journey was much like one described earlier. Maury had also encountered a Giant who had shared with him a tale about a special amulet. He had also met a wise old man who had instructed him on matters that brought him much new knowledge. And, at the end of it, he too had found his way to a strange but familiar island where he had been greeted by a group of strangers whom he soon realized were individuals that he actually knew.

As with many adventurers, Maury loved to travel and on this day he was preparing to set out on another journey. As he was about to launch his small craft, a woman approached him and asked if she could join him. Maury barely knew this woman as she had only just arrived at this island a few days earlier. She too had been travelling about, meeting strangers, encountering bizarre situations, and gaining knowledge for herself to bring back to her home island which was some distance away. Her vessel was now defective she explained to Maury and she wished to return to her home. But she would be willing to wander about with him until he satisfied his need for adventure and growth experiences. Madeline was her name and she was very beautiful. Something told Maury he should agree to her request and so he did, knowing full well that this could disrupt his own adventure, but accepting that it should be done.

As soon as the preparations were complete Maury and Madeline set out on their journey together. At first all was well and peaceful. The seas were calm, the sky was bright and the sun shone warmly overhead. All seemed peaceful for the moment. Neither one noticed as the storm blew in upon them. Madeline was fast asleep and Maury was also lying down, dreamily looking up into the bright blue sky. The storm caught both of them by surprise, fiercely shaking their small craft and ultimately tossing them into the water. As they swam to recover their vessel, a shark appeared and threatened their safety. Both were terrified and headed toward their vessel as fast as they could swim. Madeline fell behind and now the shark seemed focussed on her. Maury did reach the vessel and climbed back in to safety. Looking about for Madeline he could not see her. She seemed to have disappeared. Oh, indeed, what a sad state of affairs. He

barely knew her and now he was left to wonder what had happened to her on that fateful day.

As the storm blew itself out, Maury sought refuge on a nearby island shore. Here he set about to repair his craft and to mourn the loss of a friend. While he was occupied with his chores, a beautiful Goddess appeared on the beach near him. She was resplendent and all aglow while emanating a warm peaceful feeling. Maury was momentarily taken aback as she began speaking to him in soft and gentle tones and with great reassurance.

"My dear, Maury," she began. "I see you are very sad."

"Yes, indeed," Maury replied. "I was at sea with a new friend and she was taken from me by a shark. I am deeply saddened by and bitter about this event. I came ashore here to rest and to repair my craft. But now I am not so sure I want to return to the sea."

"That is understandable, my dear fellow," the Goddess went on. "You have suffered a great loss. Even though you did not know this person very well, you did find her amiable and saw that potentially she could have become a good friend."

Maury lowered his head as he heard these words. He truly did feel sad. He knew this for certain now. There was grief in his heart and a feeling of heaviness swept over him. He returned his attention to the task at hand and continued with his repairs. After advising him she would soon return the Goddess left Maury to continue his chores. Soon after she left, he decided to rest and lay down near his craft's bow. He soon was dreaming of far away places and great mysteries to be encountered and overcome.

Maury was still asleep when the Goddess returned. As he awoke, she informed him that his friend Madeline had not been lost after all but had washed up ashore on the other side of this island.

"If you come with me I can take you to her," the Goddess stated. "Just follow me and I'll show you the way."

As the two of them set off across the island another storm blew up from off in the distance, threatening once again the peacefulness of the day.

"Never mind that storm," the Goddess asserted. "We must move ahead quickly if we are to reach your friend before dark. She may be injured and in need of assistance."

As they quickly moved along, a loud crackling noise was heard from somewhere nearby. A great disturbance seemed to be afoot and Maury was visibly shaken. "What could this be?" he thought to himself, but continued to press on as the Goddess led the way. Another crackling sound was heard, and then another, and another.

"What was that?" Maury yelled out, no longer able to restrain himself.

"That was the sound of the devil at work," replied the Goddess. "He comes for those who cannot resist his sound."

"How does this happen?" Maury quickly asked feeling more nervous with each passing moment.

"Well," the Goddess began, "the devil is really a thought form that rises in varying forms throughout the world. Whenever people become frightened, they emit a vibration in their thoughts that allows him to surface. When they withdraw energy from those thoughts, he disappears."

"So how is it that he is here, now?" Maury asked.

"You must be feeling afraid," the Goddess explained. "And with your fear do you give him power, such intense power that he comes to life. You see your fear separates you from yourself and sends out a part of you to seek completion. When that part of you is based in fear, then a fearful result is what you will generate. In this case the crackling sound that has been frightening you has been the result."

"I see," Maury reflected. "So then it was my fear that generated this effect."

"Quite so," was the reply, "and when you withdraw your fear, the effect then dissipates."

"So how do I correct this particular situation?" Maury asked.

"By withdrawing your fear from the situation at hand," the Goddess answered. "There can be no danger if you release your attachment to danger. But there will be if you hold on to it."

Just then Maury let out a big sigh of relief. There on the beach up ahead sat Madeline. She was playing in the surf letting the waves wash up over her legs. She seemed happy and peaceful and, judging from her playfulness, largely unharmed. Maury greeted her with a hug and a kiss and began explaining how he had found her.

"So you were led here by a Goddess?" Madeline asked.

"That is so," Maury replied. "But she seems to be gone now," he continued as he looked about the area. " I believe she disappeared about the same time I saw you here playing in the surf."

"I know," said Madeline. "I saw her, too."

"You did!" exclaimed Maury.

"Yes, I did," Madeline continued. "When I fell into the sea during the storm, she came to me immediately and began reassuring me that all would be well."

"But I saw a shark," Maury quickly interjected.

"As did I," Madeline went on. "The shark was my fear in expressive form."

"And mine too?" inquired Maury.

"Yours to a certain extent, but primarily it was mine," Madeline went on to say. "And as soon as I saw it I began to pray. The Goddess came to me immediately and explained what I should do. She instructed me to release my fear, to breathe through it, and let it go. As soon as I was able to attend to her instructions while focussing on my breathing, the shark disappeared. By that time you had already scrambled back into the vessel and I was carried by the sea until I washed up on shore here. The Goddess stayed with me until you arrived. Then she left to greet you. After which she returned to advise me that you were here, also safe and sound. I was delighted and wanted to rush to you but the Goddess said "No," that I should wait, for you had a lesson to learn and only she could help you. I did not know until now what that lesson was, but now I realize that it had to do with fear also. Remember when you were in the water swimming for the craft, you thought the shark had disappeared so your fear at that time was temporarily allayed, and the lesson was no longer there to be had. So, on your crossing of the island to find me, you still had a lesson to work through as part of this journey and that is what you confronted as you made your way here to me. Now that you have arrived, I can see that you have experienced that lesson as well. And I thank you for coming to me, for I was extremely lonely without you."

"You are welcome," Maury replied. "I am only too happy that you are not hurt and greatly relieved that you were not lost at sea."

"And I feel that way in regards to you too," Madeline repeated, expressing her own relief in turn.

With that said the two of them sat in the sand for a while contemplating this journey, their time together thus far and their respective lessons in fear. Both realized that it was the same lesson for each of them, masked in different circumstances only. Somehow they had been drawn together to experience this lesson and to share it with each other. Both were amazed at how truly fortunate they were. Whenever they needed it, it seemed that help was readily at hand. And no matter how grim things looked, there seemed to be no end to the surprises and good fortune available to them. Their future was once again filled with exciting possibilities. What adventures would they fall upon next? Both were eager to know.

For now at least:

All Was Well in Their World

On Finding Your Self

nce upon a time there was a young woman named Mary who ventured out into the world to find her Self. Now Mary did not know that this Self was lost until, one day, an angel came to call and announced, "You, madam, are incomplete. You have need of your Self and then your Soul."

"But, sir angel," Mary protested, "why do I have need of this when I feel so blissful and content?"

"That may be the case now," the angel answered, "but the day will come when a feeling of emptiness will throb within you."

Mary continued her journey through life, enjoying all that she could. She had no concern with what the angel had said since all her needs were duly met and her life seemed no different then that of others. The day came, however, when her apparently peaceful existence collapsed in front of her. She was shocked and bewildered. How could this happen? How could this be?

"I have done all that I was supposed to do," she said to herself. "I have conducted myself as others before me. To what do I owe this tragedy?"

And the angel came to call again. "My dear Mary, would you wish to speak with me, now? I have news that will help you find your way again."

"Not now," Mary replied, "I am weary and have no energy for further pursuits at this time. Come to me later perhaps, but not now. I am grieving my losses and unsure of what I will want for the future."

So the angel departed, taking note that Mary was not yet ready for the pursuit of her happiness. She had lessons to learn, feelings to feel, losses to grieve. And apparently, she was not yet ready to receive.

Mary fumbled along working through her pain as best she could, recovering momentarily some of her former zest. But tragedy struck again and down she fell into the depths of despair, much as she had done previously. Mary was quite sorrowful now, unable to raise her head and it was she who called to the angel this time, asking him to come forward in her time of need.

"My dear angel," she cried plaintively, "I have come to that point where I can no longer move ahead and I have need of your Heart and your Soul. Please come to me and help me move forward again so I can find my way back to the Light."

And the angel arrived happy and aglow and looked upon Mary and saw her discomfort.

"My dear woman," he began, "you have certainly let yourself fall hard this time. I can see that you are in quite a state."

"That I am," replied Mary. "As true as you say, I have fallen as low as I can. I am stuck in this place and unable to move forward without your guiding hand." So the angel reached over, took Mary by the hand and helped her to her feet.

"Thank you, dear angel, for your help," Mary stated. "I believe I can go on from here."

"But wait" the angel pleaded, "I have more to offer. Is that all you require?"

"I see no point," Mary continued, "in burdening you further. I'll carry on from here on my own."

"Very well," the angel conceded and left as Mary set off once again on her own.

As Mary went on she began to realize that there would be many more struggles in front of her and so the thought came to mind, "If I asked for more, would it be there for me? Would I receive what I need after all?"

And the angel returned and looked at her and said, "All you need do is ask, my dear woman, and I will be here."

"Then perhaps you could do more for me," Mary continued, "since I do find this journey quite burdensome. I seem to be having trouble moving forward on my own. Would you please join me for a time?"

"Certainly," replied the angel, "I will accompany you as far as you like."

And the two of them proceeded on Mary's path, living and learning as they went along. Mary often did not know what to expect and had to be instructed on how to act in certain situations. She learned to express herself more effectively, to assert her needs, to ask for what she wanted and to refuse that which caused her pain. Mary learned many valuable things that helped her find her way in life. And then the thought came, "Where is my Self? Where is my Soul?"

"You mentioned that to me earlier, sir angel, did you not?"

"Yes, indeed," the angel answered, "your Self and your Soul are important companions in life, worthy parts of you to discover and actualize in order to make yourself complete."

"Yes, yes, these I want, too," Mary jumped in.

"And these you will have," the angel replied, "as soon as you take hold."

"Take hold of what?" Mary repeated.

"Take hold of your life," the angel continued. "You cannot have all that you need unless you claim it, and your Self is there to do the claiming."

"How do I accomplish that?" Mary asked again.

"By asserting how you feel, by focussing on your 'inner life', by addressing all your needs from within."

"From within?" she repeated.

"Yes, within," the angel went on. "That is where you will find your Self and then your Soul."

"You mean my Self and my Soul are within my feelings?" Mary asked. "Yes. Your Self, initially, is who you are and who you are is what you experience, and what you experience is what you express, and what you express is who you are once again."

"You mean," Mary continued, "I am me from the inside out and not the other way around?"

"That is correct," the angel answered. "What you are is inside of you. What you express is what you show of that Self. That Self resides within and you know this through your 'Heart'. Your Heart, your feelings, your experience, all guide you to that Self within and that in turn guides you to your Soul."

"My Soul you say?"

"Yes, your Soul, that place where you join with all other Souls in the wealth and expression of Life. You are here to grow and to join with others and, collectively, all of you express Life."

"Do I have my Soul now?" Mary wanted to know.

"Not yet," was the reply, "but you are close, for your Self is near at hand. And then you will soon see your Soul which connects you to all of Life. Express that Self by expressing your 'being'. Then you will see that your Soul is not be far behind.'

"Will I be complete?" Mary wanted to know.

"As complete as any lover of Life can be," was the reply. "As complete as one becomes having found their way Home and having learned to love once again."

"And the Love in my Heart will be forever?"

"Yes," the angel replied. "And that, dear friend, is what ultimately makes you whole."

And so Mary understood the entire picture now. It was her Self and her Soul that she required to be complete, to be discovered through her own Heart and not that of another, not even that of an angel. And it was her life that she was salvaging when she undertook to seek help. The angel's function, she now realized, was to serve her and help on her journey, not do this for her, for only she could travel that path. And with that thought she felt reassured.

And All Was Well in Her World

Preparations underway
For the future, go or stay
No more longing, no more sad
Just get moving, just be glad

Easy lifetime on the way
When you keep all hurt at bay
But not working for too long
Hurt returns in every song

Sing out praises, sing out love
Sing out pain, and wounded dove
Share your secrets, don't despair
Love comes after every affair

Take your clothes off, defences too
Open up that heart that's you
Surrender softly to His glow
Just decide, stay or go

When Your Heart Speaks

My heart bleeds for you right now, my son
You are wounded and lie crying inside of me
Rescue me you say plaintively
Seeking refuge in all that might be here

But alone you remain, inside of your pain
No solace to be found at this time

Bring to me your daunting fears your heart says
Bring forth also that which makes me glad
I am lost in this abyss of confusion
Where the pain seems to last and last

How did this happen? From where did it strike
This blow that took me all apart?
I failed to see it coming, I failed to notice
That it wounded me deep inside my Heart

Now I am forsaken you cry
Amidst the tears and the painful refrain
No longer welded together you say
No longer capable of flight

To what do I owe this downtrodden feeling?
To what this abysmal plight?
Did I not surrender, when I saw fit not to fight?

But no you say to me, that's not the way it be
It was you who called me out from the night

Yes I am your Soul Divine, here to make you mine
And I did answer your prayer on that flight

Could it be, you say to me, that I invited tragedy?
Could it be that is how I wanted to learn?

Yes you say in turn, you called for me to earn
That place inside your Heart so hard to find

Oh no, this cannot be, that I indeed invited thee
To make my life into such a fight

Oh yes you say to me, you did call you see
And I came to you from out of the night

I brought to you this day, a very vast array
Of problems, of challenges and delights

You selected from the above, what you thought would lead to Love
And you chose only those that caused the pain

But then I said to you, is this what you would chew?
When so many tender morsels are to be had

Yes you said to me, I thank you for the tea
But I'll take the sour grapes from off the vine

For I would rather learn, if there's no particular concern
By life's most difficult and demanding of terms

This may mean that I'll suffer, but there can be no buffer
To the One who wants to rise from within

His goal for me you see, is all eternity
And to Him I cannot say that I refuse

I honor His wish to rise, by high circumstance in His eyes
And acknowledge that this lofty height can be won

And no shame am I to take, in all that is at stake
If I proceed on the toughest path of all

For you see my friend in me, I am here to be with Thee
To learn, to burn and to sow

I cannot stay behind, for there I will be blind
And what I want, what I need, is to grow

So off I go out there, to take on every dare
To risk all that I have to enjoy

The world will wait for me, and I will dance with glee
When my journey has thus come to unfold

I cannot tell a lie, I pray that when I die
I will arrive at Heaven's gate all aglow

Having burned away the crust, of too much yearning lust
I can grow, I can grow, I can grow

So you say to me, now I can really see
What is your nature that you wanted to thrust?

You are going to Heaven it seems, on God's most golden beam
Of Light, of Love and of Joy

But to get you there, you have chosen to meet the bear
To confront him and have him be your own

This you say to me, is the path that I can see
It is the way that I have chosen to go Home

And now I understand why Your Love is so grand
Now I know you in my Heart and in my Soul

So my friend in me, you take me to the tree
Where life unfolds from the deepest source within

And We will be there too, our job to welcome you
To one of God's Oh holiest of places

The Earth you may determine, is full of pests and vermin
But oh, they can teach you so much about your life

Yes it's filled with strife, yes its pain is rife
Oh yes, by all accounts, this can be so

But who are We to say, that on this very day
You have come to life, if only to be sure

For when you set about, to rule in your own house
You could not, but through escape, avoid your rise

For there We all can see, in the light of eternity
The natural, the beautiful, and the more

The very path you chose, with tragedy and prose
Has brought you to this place inside your Heart

It is here you want to be, for all eternity
To have, to hold and to love

Oh yes We say to you, of that We can approve
We applaud your courage and your store

Where all your virtues there, have been brought upon to bear
All those challenges of which you had approved

And in your final hours, you chose to let Us shower
You with gifts, with love and so much more

For now We plainly see, and you and I agree
That your Life was to be forever yours

You took your challenges well, you rose when you fell
And you soared with every companion deed

You did not falter, no, till all was made aglow
And you soared, and you soared, and you soared

So now We all agree, that in your destiny
Your path was truly so well planned

You took the trail of pain, you chose this for your gain
And you won your prizes in the end

So who can say to you, it was not this way to do
When your Soul has commanded it thus

On this We can't refuse, for you were free to choose
And you chose that which brought you the most growth

So now We ask of Thee, is he happy, is he free?
Oh yes, by all accounts, it is so

For he would not believe, that it had to be conceived
From only one particular point of view

Yes I took the path, that brought me to life's wrath
But I grew . . . and I grew . . . and I grew

My '95

A Day in The Park

here once was a young man named Alvin who lived in a city far away from his home of origin. Alvin had travelled there to discover himself. He believed that the city offered all he could need to actualize himself and be all that he could be. Alvin was not a handsome fellow, nor was he too smart. He barely got by on both counts. But to his credit he had a heart of gold and wherever he went he tried to spread good cheer and much love.

Now Alvin, it turns out, was not a happy fellow after all. He was lonely most of the time and he suffered bouts of depression that kept him paralyzed and immobile at times. Alvin did love to watch the birds outside his apartment window, as they played in the park across the way. From his vantage point he could see them dancing about in flight, chasing each other and diving for scraps of food that were left on the ground. When Alvin was in one of his depressive states, this activity was his only solace. Otherwise he would become completely despairing and sometimes even suicidal.

One day, while Alvin was watching the birds from his window, a beautiful woman passed by and sat in the park where the birds were playing. She called to them and sang with them and offered them food from her hand. Alvin was totally captivated by her. She was undoubtedly the most beautiful woman he had ever seen and he felt a strong urge to meet her. He decided that the next time he saw her in the park he would venture out of his home and say hello.

A few days later, the woman came by again and began feeding the birds as had now become her custom. True to his word Alvin left his home to go out and greet her.

"Good day," she said when he approached. "I was wondering if you would come out and say hello. I have seen you on a few occasions watching me from your window as I fed the birds and played with them."

Alvin was momentarily held speechless. He had certainly not expected to be greeted by her, and had even wondered whether he would have the courage to say hello himself. Now it was his decision whether or not to return the greeting. "Hello, dear lady," he replied. "It is true that I have been watching you from my home across the way. I admire the way you interact with the birds and how they in turn react to you. You have a special gift no doubt?"

"I like to enjoy nature," she replied. "The natural world gives me much pleasure. I miss the times when as a girl I frolicked in the great outdoors and enjoyed my summers with the creatures of the forest."

"You are not from the city, then?" Alvin inquired.

"No, I'm not," she answered. "I am from the country, not far from here, and I came to the city to find work. I enjoy coming here to this little park where the birds gather and other small creatures scurry about."

"So, what is your name?" Alvin asked.

"I am Janine," she replied, "or Jean, as my friends call me."

"And I am Alvin," he continued, extending his hand to formalize the greeting.

"Yes, I know," she continued. "You are Alvin who used to live in the country also."

"Why, that's true," he said surprised. "How did you know that?"

"Oh, I know many things," she answered, "but first let us feed the birds."

Now Alvin was truly intrigued. Who was this woman and how did she know about him?

"Oh, well," he thought, "she will tell me soon enough."

Just then a policeman stopped by to ask about what they were doing.

"Oh we are just feeding the birds," Jean answered. "Nothing else really."

"Very well," the officer responded and carried on his way.

Other persons wandered by and asked again what they were doing.

"Just feeding the birds," Jean would answer, "and enjoying the afternoon."

Alvin was now eager to know more about this woman. She seemed so at ease with herself and everything she did. She was not at all disturbed by any questions or interruptions. She just continued enjoying her day, feeding the birds and watching the squirrels and rabbits running about the park.

Suddenly a hawk appeared overhead and all of the creatures in the park started to panic. The squirrels and rabbits ran and hid. The birds screeched in fear and flew about in great agitation. And then an aura of stillness came over the area that was truly chilling. Alvin asked, "What should we do?"

And Jean quickly replied, "Nothing really, he will soon go away. There is nothing for him here." And as she predicted the hawk soon left and flew off in another direction. Alvin's heart had been racing the whole time. He greatly feared what the hawk might do and had already run a number of frightening scenes through his mind. In each image a small creature had been either maimed or killed and Alvin shook at the thought of each possibility.

Jean, he noticed, was not at all distressed. She seemed to have a great faith that all would be well. She never failed to maintain her composure and self-assurance. Alvin was truly inspired. This woman was not only beautiful, but she remained calm at all times. She just seemed to know how to handle any situation, even those that appeared to pose a serious threat. No longer able to contain himself, Alvin pressed her for answers.

"Please, dear lady," he implored, "help me understand your approach to all these situations. You never seem surprised or shaken by anything that happens. The policeman did not disturb you, nor all the passersby, not even the hawk. You maintain that you are a country person like myself, yet I shuddered and shook in all of these situations. And when I feel really overwhelmed, I retreat, rather than face life's daily demands."

Jean looked at him and saw that he was truly confused. And so she set out to explain.

"Well, my dear fellow," she began, "there was a time when all these events would have shocked me and upset me also. When I first came to the city, I was afraid of everyone and almost everything I encountered. Now I am not at all concerned for I believe in a certain 'power' and this belief keeps me calm and well grounded."

"And what is your belief?" Alvin asked, now even more curious.

"I believe that God watches over all of us and blesses us with His grace. Through this grace we all are protected from that which might cause us harm. The eagle, for example, is protected by its great ability to soar high in the heavens. The horse is protected by its speed on the ground. The squirrel is protected by its ability to climb and to hide. And the rabbit is able to run quickly and turn with great ease. All creatures, including we humans, have certain special abilities that protect them."

"Yes, yes," Alvin quickly interjected, "but are not these creatures also vulnerable in many ways? Is it not true that many of them perish as they fall prey to those who hunt them?"

"This is true," Jean answered, "but all creatures are still protected by God's grace and are simply returned to their Source if they happen to perish. We humans, on the other hand, return to this life repeatedly in order to learn the lessons we need to grow and evolve."

"You mean we return to this planet over and over again?" Alvin asked in surprise.

"Or any place else," Jean went on "that may afford us an opportunity to further our growth. It does not seem to matter where such experiences take place, it only matters that we grow."

"I see," said Alvin. "Then how is it that some of us become confident and calm as with yourself, and others become withdrawn and depressed as with myself?"

"By our choice," Jean answered. "Our choices set us in our direction and our direction is determined by how we choose. This includes our feelings about things also. For example, we may choose to overcome a situation that presents rather difficult odds in an effort to remain true to our spirit and purpose. Or, we may choose a more unhappy course where, in retreating, for instance, we ultimately become depressed. Our choices determine these varied outcomes. This is a natural consequence of 'the law of cause and effect'. If I choose positively, I will receive positive results. If I chose negatively, I will no doubt reap negative consequences."

"Are you saying," Alvin interjected, "that by your choices you became peaceful and calm?"

"Yes," Jean replied, "as by your choices you became depressed."

"But I felt I could not help myself," Alvin protested.

"And that is a choice, too," was her reply. "Even though you may literally see no alternative than the negative consequence you are facing, it is still a choice, for without choice we would have no free will."

"I see," Alvin stated as he paused for a moment to digest her words. "Are you saying then that even unconscious choices, choices made without any notion of potential consequences, choices made out of habit or negative influences, are still choices for which we are individually responsible?"

"That is correct," Jean answered and went on to explain further. "All our actions are determined by our choices. If we choose poorly, we will achieve a poor result. If we choose wisely, we will likely improve our outcomes. This is not always certain, but regardless, we must in fact choose. At every avenue of life's challenges, we must choose."

"Then how can we learn to make better choices?" Alvin wanted to know.

"By seeking our deepest truth within" was the reply. "By focussing on that essence inside us that knows all and sees all and can guide us toward our best direction. This is our Soul, our very beautiful and wise Soul, our bridge to eternity, our link to the Divine, our essence lying at the very core of our being."

Alvin was breathless. He had never heard anyone speak like this. He was simply amazed. The more he asked, the more she explained. The more he tried to protest or object, the more she expanded on her basic beliefs. He could not refute her. She simply made too much sense. Eventually he stopped asking and just listened as she continued.

Her own story had been similar to his. She had grown up in the countryside and moved to the city to improve her chances of obtaining work. She too had felt lonely and depressed much of the time in those early days. Then one day, while sitting in a park, again feeling sad and lonely, a deer had come by and looked at her. It seemed to be looking right down into her Soul. In that instant she had known what she had forgotten. She knew that her salvation lay in reconnecting with Nature. Nature's rhythm had always soothed her in the past, in particular as a child growing up, but long after as well. Jean loved Nature and Nature, in turn, had taught her much. By returning to this root she had found her way out of her despair and back to that center within where her joy dwelt.

The same could happen for Alvin she explained. He too could reconnect with his inner Self by observing the rhythms of Nature. All things had a place and no thing was any more or less important than any other. Humans seemed to get depressed when they forgot this basic fact. Each of them has a place also and no one can fill that place for him. But without choosing to actively participate in Life his role and contribution do not get activated and his talents go to waste. "Such a shame," she said to him, "not to know you have a place. How else can you overcome loneliness than by finding your place?"

147

Alvin was mystified. He could not argue. His protests would have been wasted. He could only accept that she was right and that she lived what she in fact knew. One could not argue with the reality of her life. He listened for a while longer as she went on with her explanations. And then he interrupted to announce that he had to leave as his head was overflowing with these new ideas. He thanked her for a lovely afternoon and for sharing her philosophy. He was certain he would make use of what he had learned. Jean smiled warmly as she looked up at him. Then she began to speak once again.

"It is not every day that you can have a conversation with your Soul, is it?" And with that she disappeared.

Alvin returned to his home and set about to restructure his life. He had choices to make, new choices, choices that would lead him in a healthier direction. He did not want to be depressed or sad any longer and engulfed in loneliness. He wanted Love and he wanted Life. He was determined now to have both.

With these thoughts set firmly in his mind, Alvin set out to meet his destiny. Never again would he look back with regret and never again would he settle for anything less than the best of choices. The Light, he now knew, wished this for him and Alvin would not disappoint this call.

And All Was Well in His World

148

Remember when you fell asleep
Just before the last horizon
On your way to Grandma's house
To have her pies of raisin

Lulled you were by gentle strokes
That pulled at your sweet curtain
Drawn inside to that quiet place
Where only you heard the whisper

Soft this voice, speaking to you
Barely audible or deciphered
Lurking in that darkest place
Where you kept all your papers

Filled with secrets and precious lore
For only you to open
Grandma's house, you're at the door
Time to be awakened

All your soft said secrets spell
That you knew your purpose
But you kept it to yourself
Because you feared your service

No one needs to know it now
Lest you choose to answer
That call He gave on Grandma's day
That call you chased Him after

The Wedding

nce upon a time there lived a Princess in a far off land to which no one had ventured for a very long time. She had been banished to her room in her uncle's castle for having objected to his wishes to have her marry a young man from a neighboring family. This uncle was fiercely loyal to his tribe and would do anything to bring peace to his land. A marriage had been arranged between his family and that of a neighboring tribe in order to bring peace to the region. The uncle had promised his niece, Genevieve, also known as Genie, to be betrothed to a distant cousin who was the eldest son of that nearby family. When word of that promise first reached Genie, she was aghast. How could her uncle do that to her? She had a mind of her own and was amply capable of choosing her own mate. But she had forgotten about a promise made by her father to her uncle, his brother. Whoever should pass on first would leave full authority to the remaining brother to do as he saw fit for the health and well-being of the tribe.

Since his death, Genie's father had been on her mind constantly and she believed he appeared to her at times, especially in her dreams. On each occasion she felt he told her to obey her uncle and do as he said, all for the betterment of the whole tribe. While she was growing up Genie followed these instructions to the letter. Whatever her uncle asked for, she obeyed, and never questioned his authority on the matter. Over the years many requests had been made and responded to, all without question, and without hesitation. Now Genie had grown into a fine young woman and she was preparing herself to go out into the world. There would be suitors to meet and homages to pay, along with a variety of additional duties and obligations. But never did she imagine would she be obliged to give away the most precious thing in her life, her Self - her own true Self.

As the wedding date approached Genie grew ever more weary and tired, until she could no longer face the day. She stayed in her suite most of the time, as had been ordered, rarely to be seen, and only occasionally making herself present for meals. Her uncle repeatedly had her summoned and brought to him to discuss the impending wedding. But she usually refused to come forward and consistently refused to participate in this event about which only he seemed to care. Genie eventually became ill. She simply could not tolerate the idea of being given away without ever having had any say in the matter. How could she do this, she wondered, and still be true to her Self? She was further haunted by this in many of her dreams where her father would appear and maintain that she had an obligation to honor that holiest of vows he had made. The betterment of the tribe was to be first and foremost. Then, and only then, could one entertain any idea of personal needs and goals. Genie was continuously tortured by these thoughts and admonishments. During the day it was her uncle insisting that she do as required. At night it was her father reiterating to her that she do what was "right". Genie had no say in the matter, it seemed, and she became more despondent as the dreaded date approached.

Inside her illness Genie thought of many things. She thought of taking her own life. She thought of running away, simply taking flight. She thought she just might let herself die in the throes of her plight. She could not fathom any way out of her dilemma until one night an angel came to call. Genie was asleep at the time, tucked away in her room, far removed from the rest of the house. Her uncle was away, as were all the servants. So she was, in fact, truly alone. In her dream state Genie noted that the angel wore a special ribbon that glowed in the dark. The ribbon was blue and it melded with her costume rendering it all aglow as well.

"Why are you here?" Genie asked the angel.

"To help you, my dear," was the reply. "How may I be of service to you?" the angel went on. "I can see that you are troubled indeed."

"Yes, it is so," Genie answered. "My father comes to me in the night and begs me to carry forward the family honor. My uncle comes to me during the day and insists that I marry my cousin from the nearby tribe. I want to honor their wishes but my Soul hurts deeply and I am ashamed. For what I desire is neither of these, but my own life to lead."

"I see," reflected the angel. "This is quite a dilemma. To whom do you give your loyalty? To your Self? Or to your family? Some of whom are dead but, nevertheless, remain very much alive in your heart. You must resolve a very difficult situation indeed. To such an extent does this trouble you that you have rendered yourself ill in the process I see."

"I feel that I am dying inside," Genie stated flatly. "I feel that I am slowly slipping away. I have no fight left. My uncle has banished me to my room until I conform to his wishes. He has told me he has no need or wish to see me until then. My father comes to me in the night and again I am presented with the same requirement. No one regards my fate but from their own point of view."

"And you agree with them?" the angel asked.

"Why of course not," Genie quickly responded. "I totally disagree. But I am trapped between two powerful forces that are pulling me in opposite directions. My duty, it seems, is to save the family by contributing to the peacemaking process. My tribe needs this of me and I am told repeatedly that it is required. I, on the other hand, am sickened by this as I appear to have no say in the matter, or at least that is how it looks to me."

"It sounds as if you have many doubts," the angel reflected, "and some of these are about yourself."

"Why yes," Genie replied. "My father also taught me to be true to myself and to never sacrifice myself for another's gain, even if that meant a loss of life. He taught me that the most precious gift life had to offer was one's Soul, one's deepest Self. And never should that Self be denied. But how can this be true and the other be true as well? How can my father bring me one message after having taught me a set of values that it now contradicts?"

"This presents quite a dilemma," the angel repeated. "How do you swim between these two shores without being torn apart by their inherent contradictions? A truly debilitating dilemma, indeed."

Suddenly, a shot rang out, and a castle guard began shouting, "The Prince has been shot. The Prince has been shot." And all who could hear came to investigate. At the entranceway to the castle lay the bleeding body of the Prince who was to be Genie's husband. He had come to call but was accosted as he had approached the door. A shadow moving around in the nearby bushes suggested an intruder had perhaps brought this tragedy upon the Prince. Genie's uncle, having recently arrived, lay at the Prince's feet, begging him not to die. He knew the Prince's death would mean the end once and for all of his negotiations to bring peace to this area. A look of horror had already begun to spread across his face and the fear was very much apparent in his eyes. What assassin had brought this tragedy to his house? And Genie too was aghast for she knew of no reason why this young man should be attacked. As she made her way into the hall where the body now lay she could see for herself what a dilemma this had now become. Her uncle was beside himself with grief and worry and her husband-to-be lay bleeding on the floor.

As Genie gazed upon this scene, the angel returned to interrupt her thoughts and whispered to her, "This scene has not yet occurred, my dear one. These are only your thoughts projected forward. This is merely one possibility that can be played out as an ending to your current dilemma. Other possibilities exist as well, given your inclination to move in one direction or another. A broken and bleeding body lying on the floor of this house is merely one such projection. The Prince is not here, nor is he in any danger. Only this image of such a possibility exists for the moment. I have shown you this so you could see a possible outcome of your not choosing."

"My not choosing?" Genie repeated.

"Yes, your not choosing," the angel went on. "When you fail to make a commitment toward one direction or another, various possibilities may come into play. These exist as a function of your indecisiveness and they usually reflect your worst possible fears. On the other hand, when you choose, when you commit to a particular direction, then the images you see reflected there represent a new set of possibilities."

"I direct my own future?" Genie repeated.

"Yes," the angel answered. "By your choices do you do so."

"How do I choose then?" Genie begged to know.

"On this matter we cannot advise," the angel stated. "Free will requires that you wrestle with your dilemma until you find your own answers. But remember, making no choice is a choice, and can be filled with dire consequences, as I have just shown you. So choose well when you do so. But choose you must, for this aspect of life cannot be avoided."

And with that said the angel disappeared and Genie was once again alone in her room. Now she could clearly see the horns of her dilemma.

She had to choose between her needs and those of the tribe, or so it seemed.

As Genie pondered this somewhat further, she began to realize that other possibilities could exist as well. Each time she envisioned a choice, she could see it played out in her mind. With the knowledge gained through this process she could perhaps more easily make the best choice for all concerned. And this she in fact did later that night. The scene she envisioned saw her visiting the Prince and asking him how he felt about this wedding. And as she visualized this encounter she realized that he could likely be as unhappy as she, wrestling with the same dilemma of honoring his family as opposed to his own needs.

Genie decided to follow up on this and went to her uncle to ask for permission to visit the Prince. Her uncle agreed, happy that she was perhaps warming up to his point of view. But he insisted that, when she did go, she return within a few hours, for it would be improper to visit for too long under the circumstances.

Early the next day Genie left for her visit with the Prince. As she rode along in the direction of the neighboring castle, Genie came upon a bear. The bear stopped her and asked for directions.

"My dear Princess," he began, "I am at a loss as to where to find the best supply of honey. Which would it be, North or South?"

"Sir bear," Genie answered, "how can I, a mere human, advise you on the best path to honey. You are a bear after all and only you can find that direction."

The bear retreated and carried on his way. As Genie rode on further, an owl flew by and stopped at a nearby tree.

"My dear Princess," the owl asked, "where can I find the best morsels of food for my likings as an owl, and one who likes to hunt only during the night?"

Again, Genie replied, "Sir owl, I cannot help you. I am human after all and I know not of such matters that have to do with owls. You will have to find your own way there, as I only know of human enterprises, and even there I am not so sure myself."

The owl flew away leaving her alone again to continue her journey. And then, all of a sudden, a bandit appeared and demanded all of her money.

"I have no money, sir," she stated. "I am on my way to the Prince's castle and he is not expecting me. I have no wealth of my own, only my clothes, and this horse that has carried me this far."

And the bandit withdrew, leaving her alone once again, to carry on with her journey.

It seemed that no matter which way Genie turned she had nothing to offer these individuals who crossed her path. She could not help the bear, nor could she advise the owl. She could not even provide a mere trinket or bobble for the bandit who was far more dangerous than the rest. Why was she so insistent on pleasing her uncle and her father? The question pressed itself upon her with even more vigor now. "This is not my issue," she suddenly realized. "It belongs only to my uncle and his interpretations of my father's wishes. It does not involve me or the Prince. Neither of us has a part in this. We are only being used by those who see us as modes of exchange. In their view we can fix the problem, but the problem is not with us. A marriage is no cure for a warring heart. It is this negative attitude that must be made new."

With this realization, Genie turned her horse around to return home. She decided she could not help her uncle after all. He had to confront his own issues and only this would lead him out of the darkness and fear that lay in his heart. Upon her return to the castle this realization and her decision were explained. Genie also included a detailed account of her encounters in the woods and, in these, her uncle saw "signs" that perhaps he had been mistaken. Another approach to the tribal dilemma would have to be taken. Another path to resolving that conflict would have to be sought. In the meantime there would be no wedding, of that he was now certain.

Genie retreated to her room again, but not in sadness this time, for she had broken through to an important realization for herself, which now led her out of her plight. She could solve her own problems only, and not those of others. They had to undertake their own affairs and find answers that did not involve the unwarranted use of others. With this realization accepted she began to feel happy and alive once again. She could now feel a sense of freedom opening up inside her as well. For now it was plainly evident that all the messages she had received said one simple thing. "To thine own Heart be true, and Love will be there forever after." So from that moment on she did just that, determined now to remain true to her own "voice". And with that thought she knew inside her Heart:

That All Would Be Well in Her World.

Poetry rhymes with Self and Soul
With salt, and wounds, and healing
Poetry rises from out your heart
And sends you out mischieving

Poetry says "sing out loud,
Those funny sounds need rhyming"
Poetry speaks from out your Self
It's time to do your signing

Sign your name across your heart
And promise you'll keep rhyming
Sign your name as if it costs
Your life, as if it's pining

Can't you keep yourself on course
Without this withered "said so"?
No, you can't, because your heart
Needs rhyme to keep its tempo

Rhyme with all your true vibrations
Sing it out "allegro"
Find the rhythm that is yours
And sign "received Your memo"

On Finding Your Purpose

The Lord High God, He travels in high places
He informs all of His Life and Purpose
Then He chooses from among those who listen
A vast array of soldiers and emissaries
This He does to advance His causes and awakenings

Those who listen are drawn by His word
They are moved by the stirs deep within
This wellspring of truth drives them forward on their quest
Where they journey is where they live, and what they share

Share all that you have, let that be for certain
For in so doing do you advance His causes and delights
Let no one tell you differently about your goals and purpose
If this conflicts with your pulse within

This is, after all, your guiding beacon
To all that's alive and well, and truly matters in your quest
For you were sent here for a purpose, and not merely a test
Lest that purpose be like for many, a simple chord or turn
Rather than the symphony your Soul wants to play

Let it not be forgotten that He Who Knows All and Sees All
Sent you forth on this mission of mercy
Sent you out to awaken that Divine spark within

It is there to be your wellspring of deserved activities
Its range is to reach out to where it all began
Let this spark be your guide to His Heavenly Purpose
And let this be your beacon to His Eyes

An Invitation to Share

Look to each other as if you were looking in a mirror
If only to get a better view of yourself

You are all the same, you all have the pulse lying dormant within
Awaiting its call to rise

The call must come from you, to awaken this slumbering giant
No one can do your awakening for you
Each must do this on their own

But you can learn from each other, this sharing of the pulse
And then show each other how to be

This pulse knows no bounds, it will show you how to live
Just speak to it softly and lovingly
And then watch it rise from within

These are your tasks, my friends
The God of All Time wishes to be known and made visible
Let Him speak to you now, His time has surely arrived

Inside your Heart you know this is true
That the pulse lies buried in you
Each time you access it you bring a little more Light to the World

The World needs Light now, Oh, so desperately so

The World awaits your call

Look to The North

here once was a young man named Martin who went on a long journey to visit his Soul. Martin had always been a quiet man until one day a reindeer crossed his path. This deer had descended from the North where great wise men were said to dwell. The deer was a messenger sent by He-Who-Knows-All to inform all those who would listen of His goals. On this day the message was being delivered to Martin to awaken to certain truths within and to share this new knowledge. Martin had always been so quiet that his life rarely met with any upheaval or change. However, when this message came, Martin accepted it and off he went into the World to carry forth his mission.

Martin had been asked by He-Who-Knows-All to carry a message to all the people of the land. The message was a poem which he was to recite at every juncture in his travels. This message was very special in nature as it had been stated repeatedly over the centuries and throughout time. It was a message of Peace and Love and it went as follows:

Gather ye round my friends and neighbors
For I have news of grave importance
The Great One of God has contacted me
And asked that I repeat to you this song

Oh where can you be, you who can see
The Light and Love of God everywhere
There happens to be, at this time in history
A challenge that aims to bring us around

For you see my good friends, if the truth were to be known
There is no simple answer to be had at this time

Our paths are intertwined. We are all connected
And He-Who-Knows-All wishes to be found

Now let us see if we can determine what His true nature might be
In the systems of planets and stars that abound

We cannot know His story, if we stay bound to the Earth
And do not venture forth into the further reaches of His mind

Could it be that we, His seed, are too frightened to proceed
And discover what He has left for us to be found?

It is our task, you see, to seek out such truths
It Is up to us to find Him and then return

He sent us forth before, and gave us all we needed
So that we could learn, and love and share

When we departed then, it was to return again and again
And each time to be richer for the "travail"

But soon we forgot our nature; we forgot we were not found
And we misplaced that most important direction to the North

For there up in the sky, hangs a star that is His eye
And it can lead us back to where we are to be found

This eye we see out there is present everywhere
And helps us find our way on this His holy ground

We cannot be forsaken, if He has simply taken
All manner of precautions to help us come around

There was a time you see, when we thought we could enjoy
All manner of glory in distances that abound

But we soon learned of our nature, that we were easily frightened
And our assuredness and curiosity ran aground

As we began to look about, for the truth in what we saw
We fell asleep and slipped into our despair

Because the Eye that once guided us, had lost its luster dear
We wound up wandering aimlessly all around this sphere

Now the message I have to bring, is of good news I am told
The message is that We can again be found

We have to look inside now, for that eye we saw in the sky
And there our treasure, I am assured, will be found

The Eye inside is our connection, to the Holy Divine Fire
It is our link to all that's eternal and true

We have only to look about us, to know that we are observed
And that our fate is not so random after all

There is a purpose in everything, a pattern to be sure
That sets us upon our path that is true

This Eye we hold inside is our beacon of Light and Love
It will take us back to Him who is aware

We cannot know for certain, if our aim is true or perfect
But we can know of our purpose through our Soul

This Eye I speak of, is the Soul my friends, tis true
It is of Him who incarnates His Love in Us

His dwelling is Forever; of this there is no doubt
No life exists without Him, that's for sure

He honors us our wishes, our task it is to listen
And bring forth that which whispers in the dark

This deeper inward dwelling, which hides all kinds of secrets
Is the place where wonderful treasures are to be found

For He who dwells within us, speaks freely from this chamber
Advising us of our purpose and our path

Why would He be non considerate, of all our needs and wishes
If these were not part of His grand design

He does not ignore our needs, nor deprives us of special benefits
Since all of these have a purpose in the Plan

The Plan He has is certain; it requires all of us to participate
As He cannot bring it about on His own

He created us to be with Him, and to bring forth His sweet glory
So that all manner of life and purpose would abound

There is no other purpose, than to be in His service
To ensure that all forms of Life are to be expressed

For without our participation, our Lord He has no Nation
And no life nor love will be here found

And so you see my friends, your purpose is very important
To Him from Whom all Life has been derived

He has no need of service, unless it's part of a purpose
And that purpose is that Home can be regained

Now listen to me all ye people; we have a reason to rejoice
We have laughter; we have a purpose; we have a voice

The voice we give to Him, is not to be growing dim
But to shout louder the praises that He be blessed

He gave us all His Energy; He gave us all His Love
And in so doing, asked only that it be returned

The great cycle of Life requires, that there be giving and receiving
So that all could be nurtured and thus served

There is no other purpose, than to bring about this service
To ensure that our voice be loudly heard

Let us now sing out His praises, as we chant our Forever song
Let us shout out so that all can be informed

We have whispered for too long; we have held back our tones
And our voices have grown weaker each passing day

We were never lost, only asleep, and now we are awakening
We are all part of His great plan and scheme

There is no use pretending, that we are alone any longer
This has never been the case, to be sure

Our egos only thought so, because they lived in fear
It was they who believed that we were alone

But this was not the case, that we were ever abandoned
No, it was never true that we were left on our own

So my friends in our rejoicing, we can all know for certain
That our Lord has come forth to take us Home

He reaches out from the Heavens, and up from in our Hearts
To touch us and have us be His own

He is not jealous of our delights; He is not saddened by our plights
He is only too pleased to have us all come Home

So gather up all ye belongings, and point yourselves to the North
For the star up there beckons us to go on

To His Castle in the Sky . . . To His unwavering Eye
Let us venture forth at last, and go Home

A Warrior's Life

nce there was a young man named Oliver who swore an oath to uphold the laws of his land. Oliver was a soldier who had travelled far and wide and fought in many battles, all in the name of "glory" to his Country. In his land one achieved greatness by going into battle. The battlefield was a place of honor and the more enemies you killed, the more honor you obtained for yourself and your Country. Oliver had done well for himself, having been victorious in many such battles, having killed or maimed many of his country's enemies and having brought much honor to himself and to those whom he served. His tour of service was now at an end and he was reaping the benefits of being a war hero in a land that valued this type of accomplishment. All who knew Oliver respected and honored him. He was revered wherever he went.

One day while travelling about his city, he came upon a little boy. This little boy was fatherless and made his living by begging in the streets. Oliver felt sorry for this boy and gave him some money. He also shared with him his tales of glory and military accomplishment. The little boy listened and seemed captivated by every word, but actually, he was more concerned with the money he received so he could buy himself some bread. As the days passed Oliver met the little boy on several occasions, each time telling him stories, each time giving him money for bread. Then the day came when the little boy could not be found. Oliver looked for him everywhere but to no avail. No trace of him was to be found anywhere.

Oliver, dejected now, stopped trying to look. He was sad for he had lost a friend. He had lost an outlet for his stories, which was also painful, because in the telling of them he could relive his days of glory. While wandering around the neighborhood where the boy was last seen, Oliver came upon a little girl, equally ragged, equally alone and without anyone to look after her. She begged him for money to buy bread and that he provided, but only after sharing with her one of his stories of the battlefield. She listened intently of course, but, once again, only so she could receive the money in the end. Oliver, for his part, was relieved to have another friendly ear listen to his tales of glory. The days passed and the encounters continued. The little girl would appear, Oliver shared a story, then he gave her money for bread.

The day then came when the little girl no longer appeared. She too had disappeared, leaving Oliver without a friend to whom to tell his stories. In the end Oliver no longer preoccupied himself with worry over this. He concluded that such individuals would come and go in his life and another one would be along shortly.

One day, while wandering through a park, Oliver came upon a dove whose wing was broken and who, therefore, could not fly. Oliver picked up the dove and took it to his home. He nursed it back to health and released it once it could fly again. He felt happy. For the first time since the children had come and gone from his life Oliver felt good about himself. He could not share his stories with the bird but he could help it regain its health. For this he was truly grateful and pleased. There were few such pleasures in his life, and not many since his days of war.

Oliver began to reflect on this now. What was it about war that made him so happy in the first place? Was it the glory? Was it the winning? Was it the adventure and excitement? He could not answer these questions for himself until one day the dove reappeared at his window and began to speak to him.

"I am here, sir, to thank you for saving my life. You brought me back to health and then released me, and for that I am grateful."

"I was only too pleased to help," Oliver replied.

"Yes, I realize this," the dove went on, "but why then are you so sad at this time?"

"Well, you see," Oliver answered, "when I was a warrior I had a purpose. My purpose was to serve my country and bring glory to myself in the process. I did this well for many years. Until recently that was all I had in my life. When I returned from the last campaign, I was determined to find something new for myself. I knew that I was done with warring but what would I do now. All I've known in my life is the battlefield, the rules in my country and its laws. All of these I honored to the best of my ability. But then shame came upon me during that last battle. I had killed many men that day. Good, brave, strong men who were there to uphold the laws of their land, who saw me as their enemy as I, in turn, saw them. In the end I was victorious, but to what avail? I am no longer happy with that warring part of myself. I began to realize this when I met the little boy. He seemed eager to listen to me at first, but only, it turns out, in exchange for money to buy food. I, on the other hand, needed him more than he needed me. I needed to share my stories, for that was the only way I could keep those memories alive. They gave my life value and, without the opportunity to share those stories, I was left feeling lonely and bereft of meaning in my life. With the little girl it was the same thing. She listened, too, but, once again, only to obtain money for food. When you came along I had a different mission. I could not share my stories with you, but I could mend your broken wing, and this gave new meaning to my life. I hope you can understand what it is I am sharing."

"Oh I believe I do," the dove stated. "Your life had been meaningful only when you could defend your country in battle and kill its enemies. But in the end you realized that those enemies were similar to you, living the same kinds of beliefs and dying for them. Now that the battles are over you are uncertain as to where your life will take you. The past you understand, but the present is different and somewhat confusing. The present requires you to be something other than a warrior - a healer perhaps?"

"Yes, a healer," interrupted Oliver with some excitement. "Perhaps that is what I am to be now. But how does one become a healer when one has spent one's entire life as a warrior?"

"That is a good question," the dove replied. "How does one change from one mode of being to another that is its complete opposite?"

"You see what I mean," Oliver continued. "I find this all so confusing. I knew how to be a warrior because that is what was expected of me. But now, if I am to change, and I do wish to do so, how do I accomplish this? How do I become what I can now perceive is the opposite of what I was?"

Just then an angel descended onto the scene.

"I have heard your prayer, sir," the angel stated, "and I am here to instruct you on your new manner of being. Do you wish me to go on?"

"Yes, yes, by all means," Oliver quickly answered.

And so the angel proceeded to explain. "When you served your country, you did so for reasons that you believed to be good. Your country had laws which you swore to uphold and you did so to the best of your ability. When that was no longer required, you retired from the battlefield and came home. You did not know what to do, so you wandered around your city. You met the little boy and then the young girl and relived your glory days with them. That helped you for a while. But when you lost them, you yourself felt lost once again. When the dove appeared, injured and in need of help, you found a new purpose. You devoted yourself to its needs without consideration for your own. No exchanges were made, no stories were shared. Only a helping hand was extended to a creature in need. That, sir, is the essence of glory, or, more accurately, Grace – to help another without considering one's own needs and wants. To bring exchange into the process is to cheapen its value. When you paid the children to listen to you, you could never come away satisfied. They had no need of your stories, they needed only bread. The dove, on the other hand, was in need of your help, help that only you, experienced in the ravages of war and in mending wounds, could provide. You did so and you felt good. You did not cheapen the gift by adding a story. You simply engaged in a selfless act that helped another who couldn't help itself. Do you see the difference?"

"Yes, I believe I do," Oliver answered. "I believe I can see that, when I truly give of myself without expectation, I am rewarded with that feeling of Grace."

"That is correct," the angel went on, "that feeling of Grace. And so, sir warrior, is that feeling different from, or similar to, the feeling of Glory?"

"Why it is quite different," Oliver answered. "Yes, of course. Grace is an inner feeling and Glory comes from without. In Glory I am serving others or upholding some mysterious laws that I don't even understand. But in Grace I am serving my inner Self when I provide aid to another. No Glory on the battlefield has ever equalled this. Oh what joy I feel in this feeling. So that is the meaning of selflessness. Oh what a wondrous feeling."

"Then you have learned your lesson well," the angel went on to say. "The Lord High God will be very pleased. He is greatly reassured when one of His dominion is returned to himself and to the service of the higher good. His praises be upon you." And with that the angel retreated from the scene.

Oliver was left to ponder his life experiences. He started out as a warrior, a destroyer of life, the purposes of which he was now unsure. His present view of life leaned toward providing healing and service to others for a greater good, far greater he now realized than even he could behold. He had the children to thank and of course the dove, all teachers in this lesson on the value of life. In his heart, Oliver knew what path he was to follow. And that path led him toward Grace now and not toward Glory. Glory belonged to his past and the requirements of an earlier time. Grace belonged to his present and to his future, and promised to be far more fulfilling than anything he had previously experienced. And with that thought he felt good.

And All Was Well in His World

We know not where we go sometimes
We know not our true shadow
It lurks inside our breast it seems
It falls out from our mantle

This quest we're on is not oft scoured
By those who chose their station
From these mere lots, life us derived
And not them that make a Nation

Those that need be grown again
Are of stuff that makes us do
What our Selves and Hearts they want
And what our Souls need new

Rejuvenate your heart my friend
Give it one more wrapper
Don't ignore or hesitate
You'll regret that, fore and after

Because your fate is tied to His
Sound out your own refrain
That's His note inside your heart
And that is why you came

Sing it loud and sing it plain
Don't hold back any longer
He has you now inside His gate
He has you forever after

Just relax and let it come
It knows its way out there
You see this note was written once
When you came here prepared

The Rescue

I n a land far away, during another time, lived a young woman named Lisa. Now Lisa had been seriously ill for a very long time. No one had been able to help her. Many magicians and doctors and soothsayers had been called to her side but to no avail. The illness seemed unrelenting and this young woman now lay dying.

Some distance away from Lisa's home lived another individual whose name was Armand. He was from a far off land of which few people in Lisa's home area had ever heard. This area, strangely enough, was called Lapis land, which meant "Forever." In this land apparently, all persons seemed to live forever, at least most of its inhabitants were known to achieve a very ripe old age. No one actually died in Lapis land. They just transformed themselves into another form of essence, that is, from the "material" to the "spiritual." Armand, who was known to have exceptional healing abilities, had a reputation that had spread far and wide.

Armand had been summoned from his homeland by Lisa's father, who had heard of him and his special abilities. The request for aid had been delivered by a courier and Armand quickly responded. When he arrived at Lisa's home, he was immediately escorted to her bedside and was asked to please help in any way he could. Lisa was lying asleep, appearing to be barely alive and barely able to breathe. Armand examined her closely and then shook his head.

"This woman is no longer with us," he said. "She has gone to the land of the dormant ones where spirits remain suspended until they are either retrieved, or doomed to wither completely."

Lisa's father was aghast. "Do you mean she has died?" he asked plaintively.

"No, sir," Armand replied. "What I mean is that she has drifted into that nether world between Life and Death where she can no longer hear us."

"Then how do we reach her?" the father wanted to know.

"I do not know just yet" was Armand's reply. "I must ponder this for a time and I will return to her later."

Armand was led away and taken to a room in the house where he could meditate and collect his thoughts. In all his experience no such situation had ever arisen. He had never seen anyone lying so sick and disabled as Lisa. Back in his homeland everyone seemed to remain relatively healthy and happy and were able to express this state of contentment with more or less great ease. Here he was faced with a young person who had lapsed into unconsciousness for no apparent reason. Her will to live had left her, it seemed, and he was uncertain how to proceed.

As Armand continued to ponder this dilemma, he slipped into a meditative state where he could allow his spirit to soar. In his reverie he travelled back to Lapis land to try and understand more clearly why life there seemed so blissful. In his state of suspension Armand could see all his countrymen in their spiritual essence. He could see how bright and glowing that essence actually was. He could also see how that essence was activated through various modes of expression and how it glowed even more brightly when individuals made caring contact with each other. As he studied this phenomenon, he began to understand Lisa's illness. In her land, he had noticed, there were few such expressions of caring contact. The subjects there were quite closed. These individuals barely touched each other, and young sensitive people like Lisa were prone to wither inside from this neglect, with some form of illness often following.

Returning his attention to his current surroundings, Armand continued to ponder this question in his conscious state. Within a very short time Lisa's father burst into the room. "She has taken a turn for the worse," he announced breathlessly. "We need you right away." Armand rushed immediately to Lisa's room where he found her gasping for breath. All family members in the room wore expressions of deep concern. The whole family stood transfixed in the face of what they saw before them. Armand knew he had to act quickly. He had a coachman summoned and asked that the house's fastest horses be prepared and attached to a large coach. These he would require immediately for a quick trip back to Lapis land. He explained to the father that he now needed certain special tools to help Lisa and these could only be found in his homeland.

Armand's requests were quickly granted and the coachman arrived at the front of the house with a large coach led by the house's finest horses. Armand sped off in the direction of his homeland. Within a few hours he had completed his mission and returned with a coach full of children from Lapis land. Lisa's father was relieved to see him return so quickly and expressed his continued appreciation of the efforts being made. Armand quickly acknowledged the father as he instructed the children to follow him up to Lisa's room. Once there, he invited them to surround her bed. As the children gathered around the bed, they joined hands to form an uninterrupted circle. Armand joined in with them and asked that all persons in the house please be silent while he and his group prayed. With heads bowed, he and the children began reciting the following prayer.

Oh Great One from above
Please help us on this day
One of Your Souls is lost
And we are here to pray

We ask for her recovery
We ask for her return
We ask that she be brought back to us
So she can once again learn

We beseech you Oh Great One
To help us with our plan
It is our goal to rescue her
And have her back in hand

We know that she is lost Great One
We know that she is in pain
We know she cannot hear us yet
But soon she may again

Please pass our message on to her
That Love indeed here reigns
There is so much for her to do
Back on this Earthly Plane

Please help Oh Great One we beg You
Convey our message forth
Have Lisa know that's why we're here
And she's free to choose her course

And with that said, all of the children from Lapis land began to hum a song from home. The song was of Love and Spirit and the delights of being alive on this Earth. It was about the happiness and worth of sharing together and of giving and receiving in kind. They continued their chant well into the night, long after all in the house had retired to their rooms, exhausted from the day's ordeal. Armand himself had grown extremely weary but maintained the vigil well into the night. The children, never tired and sang their songs until the early morning.

When daybreak came, only the stillness was noticeable, as all sounds in the house had stopped, except for a raspy cough coming from Lisa's room. Armand had been asleep for a while and was the first to be awakened by the sound. All the children, of course, knew its meaning and once again surrounded Lisa's bed while she struggled to awaken. She coughed a few more times and then slowly began to open her eyes. There all around her stood the children who had sung to her throughout the night. As she looked out at them to study their faces they reached out to her and touched her, much to her surprise. But it felt so good she could not object and it was then that she saw the Love in their eyes.

Lisa continued to soak up this loving attention as Armand proceeded to examine her. He could see for himself that she was back with them now. She had returned from the "land of the lost". Her father then appeared on the scene and let out a cry of joy. He was so pleased to see his daughter awake that he momentarily forgot himself and hugged Lisa as tightly as he could. All members of the family were now back in the room eager to see what was happening. They initially appeared taken aback by the father's behavior but not one of them made any attempt to object. With Lisa now returned to them they were beginning to appreciate the methods of touch displayed by Armand and the children. They concluded that this process was indeed the "medicine" that had returned Lisa to consciousness and they were only too pleased with its success.

As the hours passed, Lisa was fast becoming more alert. She began to talk and asked for food and something to drink. A supply of treats was rushed to her and she showed a good appetite. Then her father, now composed again, asked her where she had been and Lisa proceeded to explain.

"My dear father," she began, "I had left the land of the living to travel far away from here. My heart had been aching for such a long time that I felt I could no longer stay. I went to a place where only spirits roamed and sat there wondering what to do. In this place I felt no pain, but no other feelings either. I sat there, numb, until this beautiful sound reached me. It was the sound of these children singing and it struck a chord deep inside my heart. I suddenly felt the urge to return to my body, so I came back to see what was happening in this room. As I reentered my body, I again felt the pain that I had originally left behind. But I also felt the Love in the room and I knew then that I was safe. I am truly glad to be home again. I am grateful for this life. But, I also need to advise you, that I may leave again if I feel it is too painful to stay. I needed to be touched you see. I needed that warm contact so very much and now I see clearly why I must have it. For without that warm personal contact I know I will wither and die."

Lisa's father nodded his understanding. He had seen for himself the power of touch, of Love in action. He tried to explain to Lisa that it was never a case of him or his family being without Love; it was more a matter of not knowing how to express it. Now that they all had this valuable lesson, he was certain that they could begin putting these new ways into practice. And perhaps Armand might stay behind for a time and instruct them further, for surely all would want to participate in this learning. As Armand nodded his agreement smiles broke out everywhere. There was magic in the room now, it seemed. The Power of Love had entered their midst and all could feel Its presence.

The Power of Love had spoken Its truth through the prayers and chanting of the children. Through their innocence and openness the Love flowed freely. They carried the magic that was now present all about this house. They had brought it forth and held it intact. Lisa's father and family showed their gratitude by the smiles on their faces and the kindness in their eyes. They were all pleased to know this truth. And with that acknowledged, life returned to normal again in Lisa's home, but with one very important difference. The lessons of Love were now being taught and learned and all were beginning to express this truth. And when Armand felt he was done with his instructions he then happily returned to his Home. For he knew in his heart that his task here was now complete.

And That All Would Be Well in Their World

A Letter from Santa

Oh gather ye round all my children
For I have a tale to tell of the dawning of man
He came to this Earth a long time ago
To celebrate this life that he was given and that had been blessed

Oh what wonders befell him as he ventured forth on the Earth
To discover his being in all that mattered
It was never meant to be difficult this journey through time
Only a gentle romp through the woodlands, across the prairies
    and the plains

Do not despair, my fragile friends, for you have only gone
    astray temporarily
He who knows all and sees all is here to guide you back
To that gentle place within where the poetry of your Soul resides

I have written many stories and poems to you over time
To advise you of this sacred place within
You faltered on your journey outward and failed to notice those signs
So I came to you as often as I could, in prose, in poetry and in rhyme

Each year at this time you remember me softly
In the heart of your yearning womb
You can feel that presence sublime, pulsing within your frame
More alive at this time than throughout the year

We of the ethereal realms reach you better now it seems
For your hearts are more open and we are easier to find
You receive us because you want us and we, in turn, find our
    way to you

Have you ever wondered how this all started?
Where it began this special time?
You call it Christmas; we call it Love
In our world it makes no difference, as long as one feels
    the pulse inside

Remember when you were young and, oh so eager you were then too
Awaiting Santa's reindeer to appear on your roof
You believed then so easily in the power of the mind
You never doubted that He would arrive

Your parents helped with the story, also taught to them in their youth
And so on, and so on, all the way back in time
Now you await your truth again, in the eyes of the children before you
They are here to remind you of what you once knew

The Power of Love has existed since before time
Since before there was an Earth or Heaven above
The Power of Love insisted that it be known through time
So this purpose of yours came to be born

So many of you chose to come on this journey through time
To learn all that you could about Life

Here on this Earth you can see afar
Out to the planets and the stars suspended in the sky
They teach of vastness, of triumph, and of destiny too
They teach you to dream and to look way beyond whom
  you think you are
These beacons of Light, you can take deep into your heart
And rekindle the flame that once burned bright

You are great, you are My sacred ones
Sent forward from the Light
Here to learn "what can you do" to spread this message
That all is really right with this world
In spite of all the troubles that lurk about

You see, this eternal flame that burns brightly from within
Is not ashamed of its presence, to have itself be known
Its power is eternal, It is not shy
To be expressed is all that It asks

So on Christmas morning, when you awake
Remember this message from deep in your Soul
You are not lost, you are not forsaken
You are to be found where your feelings are told

There in your Heart center, where truth breaks to the surface
There can be no mistaking that He has taken hold
And His message is not to be forgotten
For it is of the greatest story that has ever been told

When each of you surrenders to this guiding Light within
Another star lights up the sky to cast its beam into the "forever void"
Pushing back the darkness a little further
Each time one of you finds their way Home

Isn't it a great story that you all get to play a part in?
A piece of living history that unfolds itself through you
You are of the Light Everlasting
You are a beacon of His Love
You are a star in His "forever army"
Of His Love, and purpose, and oh yes, so much more

Do not be ashamed of your Being any longer
It is sacred; that you must know without a doubt
He does not cast Himself in rubble, or in stone
Only into the hearts of those whose purpose can be His own

This is Our tale of Christmas, Our message we give to you
In a package that has shaped itself through your history
Each year we bring to you another such message
To be added to the vast annals of unfolding time
Teach your children this truth of the Light Everlasting
Show them that It resides within

Take no stock in what others tell you
Of this or that not being the true path
Only theirs, or so they say

The true path for all is illumined by one's Soul
And that Soul was His to begin
Now it is yours to take you forward on your journey through Life
To learn and then teach what truth you know

Everyone has purpose, and love and magic too
Everyone has meaning in the Grand Design
To be sure, that is His Way
To provide that which is needed to sing His praises
Throughout the annals of time

To sing His praises is to sing your own
For you are of Him who has sent forth His Son
His Son is you, you see
And you are His to be sure
Till the end of time, and of course, beyond that as well

As We bid farewell to this magical mystery
In prose, in poetry and in rhyme
We return to where We began, the very first Christmas
Somewhere near the dawning of time

Merry Christmas We say to you all
From Santa ... and from ... the Divine

When you were young life pressed on you, from nightfall to day break, a series of dreams designed to bring out of you a part that was lost in time. There was no need to fear these dreams, they were only His silent way of reaching you as shadows fell. And while you slept away the day, these dreams were noble and sublime. They told of tales about you. They told your past, your present then, and your future to be discovered soon. You knew not what these messages meant, only that they spoke to you in a language undeciphered yet, but a language that was His above all. Now you rest at night and dreams still come it seems, to frighten you, and awaken you, and inform you of what you are. Listen close to these rare gems. As letters, open them soon. Learn to read your mail my friend, it may now be past due.

A Bird in The Hand

here once was a man named Eugene who wanted to sail by himself across the ocean. Now Eugene very much liked to sail. He was quite accomplished in this craft, and this was well known in his region. There, scores of young men had learned to sail, much as he had, but none of them wanted to venture out too far from their familiar area. Eugene was different. He wanted to experience the unknown. The further reaches of the sea, lying just over the horizon, intrigued him to no end. He would dream endlessly of venturing forth and discovering what lay "just over there."

The day came when Eugene was ready to set out. His sails had been set, his craft was in good repair, and the winds were favorable indeed. Just as he was about to set out a bird flew overhead cackling out a warning of dangers ahead. Eugene would have none of this. No cackling bird would stop this adventure. He was determined to continue on his course. As his tiny craft set out a storm rolled in with dark menacing clouds overhead and heavy seas swelling up. The bird, with its warning cackle sounding, flew over him once again, repeating its advisement that only dangers lay ahead. Eugene once more paid no heed and proceeded on his way.

The storm raged for days it seemed, until finally it blew itself out. At this point, Eugene was far out to sea, far from where he had originally set out. When he looked back, he could only see the tiniest speck of land. But out ahead and, for some unknown reason, now much to his dread, lay the wide-open sea. Eugene knew that he had chosen this path, but nevertheless, fear took him over, in spite of that awareness. At this moment he could not understand why he held to his plan when all signs about him appeared to advise against it. As he contemplated this, his mind drifted back to the life he had just left behind prior to setting out on this journey.

Beside being an accomplished sailor, Eugene was also a master craftsman. It was widely known that he could fashion all kinds of instruments and machines to meet the purposes of those who required his designs. In his efforts to achieve the ultimate in technical mastery he had invented a machine that could foretell the future. The residents of his area had been intrigued by this and had sought him out to take advantage of this unique application. Also, many persons had travelled from far and wide to be

187

advised of their future, such was his reputation. Eugene would hook them up to the machine, and there it would be, much to their delight, their future told.

Eugene eventually had grown tired of this practice. He had become tired of simply serving people their future fortunes. He had wanted something different for himself and no dire warnings about dangers ahead were going to stop him. That was why he had set out on this journey, because surprises, and not predictions, were what he wanted to behold. He had also decided that he would destroy his machine prior to setting out, and had informed all in his region that this was his plan. He was not to be dissuaded, he had warned them, and would hold firm to that stated intention. Many whom he had served over the years had bemoaned his decision.

When the machine was done with its last prediction Eugene destroyed it as had been his plan. Its final prediction was for a magician friend who lived in his area. This fellow had been known to take a wide variety of chances in his life, but over time, had become dependent on Eugene's "future telling machine". As Eugene lay in the bottom of his craft, all these thoughts swirled around in his mind. He was remembering now why he had set out on this sea journey and why he had left everything behind. His magician friend was sad to see him go, as were many of the individuals who had lived near him. They too, had come to depend on him and his inventions, "too much so," he thought. "Now they must go it alone," he went on, "as I am also doing in this tiny craft."

The sun beat down on Eugene's small vessel as the winds became tired in their work. All was still about him now and he had nothing to do but wait. That annoying bird appeared again overhead, cackling and menacing with apparent glee.

"You will be destroyed," it shouted. "You will be destroyed and then you will see."

"See what?" Eugene wondered. "Why is this bird nagging me in this way? I have no need of its incessant cackling and its warnings of doom laying ahead." Finally, Eugene shouted back. "Away with you, damn bird. You are an annoyance and of no value to me."

"Oh you will see," cackled the bird once again, "you will see."

Just then the winds picked up again and swept Eugene further out to sea. Now there were no tiny specks of land anywhere to be seen, no matter in which direction he looked. All about him was water now, while he, in his tiny craft, tried to hang on.

"Oh, here I will perish," he thought to himself. "Of this I am assured. For I know not my direction any longer and have no idea which way to go. My machine could have helped me now, but it has been destroyed. My magician friend could also be of help, perhaps, but he is beyond my reach. To where do I turn in this hour of need, in this forsaken place that I have put myself?"

"That is why you are here," cackled the bird from overhead, "to find out that of which you are made."

"You seem to have much information for me" Eugene yelled back. "Can you tell me then what lies ahead?"

"Yes, I can," cackled the bird, "but that is not the way to have this end."

"What do you mean?" Eugene shouted. "I have come on this journey to find my way without the usual guides. I in fact had hoped to learn something new about myself, something I could not predict from my past."

"And you will," cackled the bird, "and you will."

Just then Eugene came upon another small craft that had drifted in from his right. This vessel had no one aboard, just a message painted on its side.

"To Whom It May Concern," the message began, "if you find this craft please have it returned to its proper owner, who has somehow gone astray. He seeks Heaven on Earth and to this end he will leave no stone unturned. It will be unfortunate though if this craft is found empty, for that will mean that he has lost his way again."

Signed, "The Emperor Has No Clothes"

Eugene was struck deeply by the significance of this message. Slowly and deliberately he tried to understand what it meant. If one sets out without a purpose in mind, other than to be rid of the past, one can wind up anywhere at all. And more than that, of what value is any purposeful result if that purpose was not yours to begin with. So the message was telling him something of extreme importance, but he could not fathom it entirely just yet.

While he continued to puzzle over this, the bird returned overhead to advise him once again. "You are not lost now, my son. You are indeed found. Of this you can be certain."

"How can that be?" Eugene asked.

And the bird repeated. "When you are lost and know it not, then you are lost, and that's for sure. But when you are lost and wake up to this fact, then you are found, and that is so."

Eugene pondered this for the next while as his craft drifted lazily across the sea. Then a speck of land appeared up ahead and Eugene sailed toward it as best he could. Soon he had landed on its shore and began looking around. Nothing appeared familiar. But the bird overhead kept calling to him. "You are found, you are found, and you are no longer dead."

"I am found?" Eugene thought. "What does this mean?"

"It means that you are no longer dead," repeated the bird, who was now standing at his side. "Have I not followed you every step of the way and advised you correctly of what was ahead?"

"Yes, you have," Eugene conceded. "But how did you know what was ahead for me?"

"I am your Soul," replied the bird. "It is my duty to advise you on your life. You have no need of 'future machines', or 'magicians', or the like when you have me at your helm. With your Soul at your side you can never be lost, and that is true."

"But why are you so annoying at times?" Eugene wanted to know.

"I am annoying only at those times when you think you know everything and have it all, when you think you can decide without consulting the charts, the stars or the Lord. That is when you are most lost my friend and that is when I seem most annoying to you. But when you surrender to the pulse within, then I no longer need to rattle your bones. For you will listen now to that golden pulse that sets you forward on your own true path. So do not be afraid to look inward and gaze upon that beautiful golden bow. For there you will hear a prayer that is kind and sets you on your way Home."

Eugene now knew that what the bird said was true. He knew it in his Heart and in his Soul. For there it was revealed to him, and no longer could it be concealed, his most precious and glorious of goals. This journey he had taken was simply an adventure in finding "himself", because he had truly been lost. Now that he understood this, he no longer felt afraid and he gave thanks to his new found friend, his Soul. And from that time on it could truly be said:

That All Was Well in His World

Are we to know this path of ours
From only this one source?
The sign inside says "work ahead"
When do we finish this house?

Construction all around us borne
A nasty set of works
No time for waste or hesitates
No time to sleep or quirks

We must now know our part in this
To open up the chore
Grow in there your own new lair
Grow inside your store

Seek the shadows lurking now
In your house made do
By your own rise, you too design
A house that's yours and true

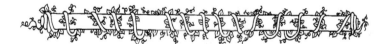

A Friend Indeed

nce there was a man named Arthur who ventured forth in his life to seek fame and fortune. Arthur was a strong believer in the mysterious and the uncommon but he was reluctant to seek these as he had heard too many stories of upset and disappointment in their pursuit. In his adventures Arthur was given to meandering around aimlessly until he came upon an opportunity to advance himself. On one occasion he discovered an old abandoned castle and so he set up housekeeping. He fancied himself as Lord of the manor for a time and amused himself with all manner of fantasies and illusions that saw him as greater than he actually was. On another occasion, Arthur came across a derelict sailing vessel lying off the shores of a great lake, and there he pretended to be a great seafaring captain, a discoverer of New Worlds, an adventurer on the high seas. Arthur had no end of amusing himself with such fantasies and, wherever he went, opportunities to do so seemed to abound.

One day, while Arthur was again meandering, he came upon a young princess who appeared to have lost her way. Arthur inquired as to whom she was. And she replied that she had come from a far off land that had been overrun by Warriors, leaving her family dead and her homeland destroyed. Her name was Genie and she was now lost and alone and did not know what she would do with herself. Arthur shared some of his own history and his propensity for fantasizing when opportunities presented themselves. He invited her to join him in these wanderings if she so wished. She agreed to do so for a time, if it were really no trouble.

One night, while the two of them were resting, a great tumult was heard from somewhere nearby. From their position, behind some large rocks, they could hear a great commotion coming from a camp whose fire they could see off in the distance. Arthur decided to wander over to see what was happening and advised his princess friend to stay behind. She agreed and remained hidden in the rocks. A few hours later Arthur returned, bedraggled and ragged, looking very much the worse for wear. He was out of breath and panting heavily, trying to put words together to explain what had happened to him. It seems the group he had approached were in fact a small band of Warriors who had been part of the raid on her home village and they were celebrating their great victory and acquisition of spoils. Genie was very distressed by this news. She had no idea those robbers would still be so close at hand and began to fear once again for her safety. She was recalling that, in the attack on her village, they had sworn to kill all in their path and they would leave no stone unturned until they had succeeded in so doing.

As Genie related this to Arthur, he nodded his understanding and then continued with the remainder of what he had overheard. It seemed the group was not completely satisfied with their accomplishment because one of the villagers had gotten away. And it was their sworn duty to their leader to ensure that no one escaped the massacre. The great commotion Genie and Arthur had heard earlier was related to this unfinished business. Some members of the group wanted to return to their homes while others wanted to pursue the escapee. When Arthur came into their camp, they immediately pounced upon him thinking he was their missing victim. But they soon realized their error and set him free. Now Arthur, still trembling from his ordeal as he related these events, was back with his friend.

A great discussion proceeded as to what they should do next. Genie reminded Arthur that he was not responsible for her and perhaps she should just turn herself over to the Warriors and end it all. Arthur would have none of this.

"Isn't it enough that they have desecrated your village, let alone that you would want to sacrifice yourself, too?" he asked. "You have suffered enough at the hands of those heathen Warriors. They should not take the best prize of all, a princess from the very village they have just ransacked. We must formulate another plan."

Genie was too weak and tired to argue. She felt that if Arthur wanted to help her she should surrender to his offer. Perhaps he had been sent by the gods to wreak revenge on these oppressors. "But, then again," she thought, "what can one man do?" Too tired to protest further, she decided to agree to any plans he thought up.

Early the next day Arthur arose to find that the company of Warriors had already left. He noticed also that Genie was nowhere to be found. His immediate fear was that she had surrendered herself to them. But, much to his delight, he saw her returning with a bucket of water to their camp.

"Just some water with which we can wash ourselves before we journey on," she said.

Arthur, greatly relieved, took advantage, and splashed water on his face. Genie did the same, and soon they were both ready to travel.

Suddenly they found themselves surrounded by the very Warriors from the previous night. They had not really left, only circled about the area in a surprise move until they came upon these two. Now Arthur was really frightened, as was Genie. She drew in her breath at the sight of them and then went limp with despair.

"There is no escape now," she thought. "Surely we will both die."

Just then Arthur began to sing and dance, and proceeded to prance around the campsite. He howled and hooted and made many grotesque gestures and sounds, all to the amusement and befuddlement of the surrounding Warriors. Genie sat on the ground and watched in disbelief. Had her new-found friend totally lost his mind or was this some kind of trick he was trying to pull? One of the Warriors stepped forward and asked him what he was doing.

"Oh, I am just performing the dance of the 'praying mantises' so my wife can have her baby boy."

The soldier stepped back in disbelief. "This man is a fool," he shouted. "We have no business here. Obviously his poor wife here will have to care for him as he is barely able to maintain his sanity."

Genie had already moved into the scene to try to calm her "ailing husband". "Yes," she said, "he behaves this way periodically. Too much sun, I guess. What can I say? The gods have saddled me with this one. It is my lot, it seems, to serve such a fool."

"What a pity," the soldier replied. "We will leave you to your tasks. We have a princess to hunt, and no time to waste with a fool and his wife." And off the Warriors went, in a direction to the North, as fast as their horses would carry them.

Arthur and Genie were now standing together alone, barely able to contain their laughter and their great relief.

"You see," Arthur stated, "sometimes fantasies can really bring riches. In this case, my meandering of the mind likely saved our lives."

"Quite so," Genie agreed. "I had no idea, initially, what you hoped to accomplish with all that howling and prancing. But, given the gravity of the situation, I felt I had no choice but to follow your lead."

"And well you did," replied Arthur, "for without your participation we would both surely be dead by now."

"So now what?" Genie asked? "What do we do now?"

"Well," Arthur answered, "if you have nothing better to do, then perhaps you would consider continuing with me on my travels."

"And play in your fantasies?" she asked.

"Yes, and join me in my whimsical adventures," he answered. "You have nowhere else to go that I can see and I am lonely. Perhaps together we can lend each other some company and amuse ourselves in the process."

With that agreed upon, Arthur and Genie proceeded on their way. South seemed like a good direction, for they were certain they wanted to be as far away from that travelling horde as possible. So, with whimsy in the air and a sense of adventure in their hearts, they strode off together in search of Life.

And All Was Well in Their World

When we were young and eager too
We ran as fast we could
To reach out there and then be aware
To do what we thought we should

But soon we learned not to concern
Our selves with petty grievance
'Cause our Lord saw fit to turn
Our lives sometimes mischievous

In play or work He held fast there
'Cause that's what He most wanted
A man, a child, a girl, a friend
To have all that they counted

Do not despair about your lot
It has all been taken care of
He chose you last because you cared
To have yourself be made of

The same hair's breath He told before
That created all life's pleasures
Yours in store, no need to concern
He has you in full measure

The Little Lamb and Mary

Mary had a little lamb
Its fleece was white as snow
And everywhere that Mary went
The lamb was sure to go

Now on this day, that Mary wept
The lamb was not to be seen
For it had gone off by itself
To see what it could dream

Mary vowed that one day soon
She would surely die
And on that day, she would fly away
To live her life in the sky

The lamb we hear, went on to say
It too would soon fly away
But first it wanted to discover
Its life through love and play

Mary, it seems, had done all this
And so she prepared to give way
But the lamb he wanted to try for himself
So he was determined to stay

Sometime later on, or so the story says
The lamb, he returned to God
And there he said "I'm done for now
May I have a rest and a nod?"

And God said "Yes" because He was pleased
While Mary had come Home too
The lamb now returned, they were together again
And that put a few things into view

For the lamb now knew what love had wrought
What a life could demand of you
But Mary didn't know, no quite the reverse
She had missed her chance to chew

Mary, you see, had avoided the tree
Where life could have taught her much more
She chose instead to lie in her bed
And there, not to worry, oh what for?

The lamb we understand, chose to seek and scan
And discover for himself life's great role
He did not tarry, much unlike Mary
Who gave up her chance to be whole

The lamb we can see, had sought out the Tree
Where life's fancies and challenges abound
He chose to try hard, for that was his charge
And he found a way Home that was sound

Now we cannot condemn little Mary our friend
For she could have found her way too
But fear took her over and she ran for cover
Her escape more important than being true

The lamb on the other hand, rose up and ran
Chomping at the bit, to be made new
He would have no part of sitting on his heart
For he wanted to have all he could chew

So now we see an end, to the lamb and his friend
Little Mary who sat down to brew
She fell asleep, while her lamb became a sheep
And he rose up . . . took flight . . . and he flew!

Heaven's gate is opening up
A stair that's hard to climb
Unless you've dared to declare
That you are His not mine

For I am you in shadows' hall
Where fear has oft made ground
And held you there til you prepared
To take off and be found

For you to set a time for Self
To rise and be made new
You must take hold, and yes, be bold
You must take hold of "you"

This "you" you seek is mild and meek
But it is you all the same
The person held inside your heart
The person you oft have blamed

For all your hurts and shadows lost
For all your debts made due
You are of Him Who heals all this
You are of Him, made "you"

Could This Be Me

here once was a young man who could not find his way in life. He had looked here and there, and everywhere, but to no avail. One day while browsing in a book store he came upon a unique volume written by someone he thought he knew. It turns out this someone was himself, but from another lifetime. Surprised, he took the book home and examined it thoroughly. If he had written this book, he could not see that at the moment. He read on hoping to find something familiar, but unfortunately without any success. So he took the book to a wizard to see if he could help him. The wizard told him that the book was indeed his but he could not realize it just yet because he was still cut off from his whole Self. But soon, he assured him, the young man would know for sure because he would meet someone who would confirm this for him.

The young man took the book home, sad that he hadn't received the answer he had really wanted to hear. A while later, while sleeping in his favorite chair, he had a dream. In this dream he saw himself floating in the sky. While floating along he came upon a messenger from God. This messenger told him to follow him and he would take him to a special place where answers to Earthly questions could be found. So, while floating along on his cloud, the young man followed the messenger toward this special place that glowed brilliantly in the distance. There were gardens there, with magnificent structures within them, and crowds of people milling about. They seemed to be dressed in long white robes with garlands of flowers wrapped about their heads. From his position on the cloud the young man could not tell if they were male or female. To him they all just seemed to glow.

Once he arrived in the garden area, he stepped off his cloud and followed the messenger up a hill to a special structure made of tall white pillars. These were assembled in a circle, and adorned with flowers, while open to the sky above. The messenger instructed him to stand in the middle of the structure and wait. Shortly after that, a beam of light shone down from above, directly on to the young man's head. He was astonished because he had never before experienced such a warm glow. He stood transfixed while the beam washed over him completely. Suddenly he knelt down in prayer and gave thanks because now he understood why the messenger had called him to this place. His High Self was in the beam of light blessing him with all His graces. And the young man indeed felt blessed. He understood now that his life was more than his current personality could apprehend. He understood that the boundaries of his existence went beyond that which he was usually accustomed. There was more to everything, he realized, much more than he had ever been able to appreciate.

Suddenly, the young man found himself back in his chair, in his home, holding the book in his hand. He looked at it again and realized that it indeed did belong to him in the same sense that all forms of life belonged to each other. His own universe, being small but complete, contained all the experiences of his many lifetimes and he could access these by accessing the center of his being. From there, like at the hub of a wheel with its spokes extending outward, he could see the varied directions his many lifetimes had taken as these were being reflected back to him. By finding his way to his center he could see this more clearly now. And this proved to be an amazing revelation for he could also appreciate why he had so much trouble recognizing his involvement with the book in the first place. Yes, he had penned it, but in a time gone by; yet he could claim it as part of the vastness of his experience. The Universe had provided him with an answer. It was now up to him to accept it. And this he did. And he gave thanks for the lesson learned.

And All Was Well in His World

My friends when you're alone at night
Do you prefer to love or fight?
In light of day or sweet of dusk
To whom you say "In God We Trust"?
For trust in Him is precious and few
Is this too much for one to chew?
God we know, trusts you, you say
Do you know now to whom you Pray?

On Having a Mission

nce upon a time there was a young man named Maury. He came to Earth to serve his Lord who had sent him on a mission. The lord had asked that Maury join with the World in order to learn its ways. Then he could be entrusted to serve in the highest manner possible. Maury agreed. The Lord always had a requirement that went beyond the obvious in any situation of service. In this case He entrusted Maury with a duty that could only unfold and be known at certain points in his Earthly life. Until he reached these points, he was to know no more than anyone else at that particular stage of their life. But once Maury reached a certain age he was to know all that was to be set before him.

The Lord had asked that Maury be awakened at this time to his true purpose. He would have to know this in order to carry on as required, else he might become discouraged. So the Lord told him that He loved him and that He appreciated all his hard work. At this point in his life, Maury had become quite knowledgeable in human affairs and quite diligent in his practices. He never left a task undone and always went to the limit in any matter that was asked of him. All that the Lord had wished for was there before Him. An instrument so fine anyone would have been proud of. And the Lord was, and pleased as well.

Now it was time to tell Maury of his mission. His mission, you see, was to bring about a radical shift in human consciousness. And only by knowing that shift himself could he teach it to others. Maury knew little of this shift at the beginning of his life. He behaved as others did and lived life like anyone else. But as he grew, he questioned, and soon he found himself questioning everything. Until one day, he realized, the only way you can obtain good answers to such questions was by going directly to God. So he did just that. He started talking to God directly and soon he was on his way to receiving the best possible answers to all of his questions. And God did answer as best He could for He knew that if He was to keep Maury's interest He would have to talk to him directly from now on. Because Maury was no longer satisfied with any old answer. He wanted it straight. "Tell me what you want Lord and I'll do it" was his motto. So the Lord was ready to tell him and Maury was eager to hear.

The story told to him was that Maury's task was a formidable one, to awaken the "Army of Light", to touch all the Souls of those who had been bitten by the big sleep, the secret separation that had hypnotized so many in their present environment. "So many lost Souls," the Lord would say. "How could I have lost so many beautiful Souls?" Maury listened and knew this was so, because God always spoke from His Heart. And Maury knew also what was in the Lord's Heart because he knew his own, and that too was the Heart of God.

By knowing his own true feelings would Maury know what God wanted, and where He wanted him to be. Maury was there, listening to every word, feeling every nudge, grasping every whisper. Sometimes God whispered, you see, so he had to listen carefully. But he did, and he was good at it. Because all the while he was healing his own wounds, he learned to listen to himself, and that helped him listen to God. God was right there, behind all those feelings, all those hurts, all those losses. God was right there and Maury knew it now. He knew it fully. So the message was there as well.

"Go listen to your heart," God would say, and Maury listened.

"I hear it Lord," he would answer. "I hear that pulse within. It is growing stronger now, Lord. I can feel it in my bones."

"Yes, it is," God would say, "a very strong pulse indeed."

"Thank You, Lord. I'm glad you approve. I have done my very best. All that you asked. And I can do more if you like."

"I know," the Lord would respond. "You are doing amazing things already."

"Thank You, Lord. All because of You and what You've taught me."

"Say your prayers, son," the Lord would say. "Say your prayers and listen to My voice; it is there beside your own. And I know you can hear that one now, so very well indeed."

"As true as you say Lord, I hear it."

I hear your whispers Dear, as You sing softly in my ear
I hear your poetry, as you whisper 'Come to Me'
I hear You all aglow, when You say 'to go'
I hear all of it out there, 'take on every dare'

I hear You sometimes desperately, standing by a tree
I hear You in my heart, time to stay or start
I hear You everywhere, "do not fear the bear
Trust your heart in Me, for you are soon to see
My life yours to bear, when you take on the dare

Dare to be with Me, inside every tree
Dare to be alone, there's no need to groan

All life comes to pass, by My song at last
So be true to Me, then you will all see
That your life in there, is also Mine to bear"

So the Lord He came to live inside Maury's heart, so they
could be together as had been the plan all along.
But this time consciously, is what we all can see
For Maury's place in there, was no need to despair

The Lord He is here now, do not fear His brow
Furrowed though it may be, has no heed for thee
Lest you are afraid, or sorry that you stayed

Otherwise go out there, and take on every dare
Then you'll soon discover, who it is your "lover"
That He resides in thee, and inside every tree

    Maury was pleased with this song. It kept coming into his mind.
A word here, a phrase there, all singing together the praises of his Lord.
Singing his own as well it seems, as he now knew "for whom the bell
tolled". The bell tolled for all those Souls that were yet to be awakened, for
all those still asleep. For all those that, like so many sheep, were unable to
choose their own direction, unable to feel their own pulse. When Maury
agreed to undertake this task, he knew the risks involved. The Lord had
not forsaken him and kept him informed every day. Maury had no difficulty following His mind, once he knew it was his also.
    Then the time came to put the plan into action. And that's when
Maury knew he had a new day ahead of him. No longer lulled by the past
or his own sleepiness, Maury undertook to move the plan forward by publishing the Lord's wishes in a series of books of fables designed to awaken
people's minds. All of the books were to be about this. "Wake up every-
body," they would say. "Wake up, the time of the Lord is upon us. Let us
all wake up and rejoice. His time has finally arrived."

    At the end of this tale we can see that Maury's life was only begin-
ning, as was the case with all who heard this same message in their hearts.
Maury's is only one such case, of the many who are now underway. He
was just learning what was required of him and was eager to share his new
knowledge. "The times they are upon us" he would say. And they were,
and he did:

And All Was Well in His World

The Road to Mercy

Once there was a man named Maury
Who followed his heart to the end
He chose a path of sorrows
But that was how he wanted to fend

Now Maury, you see, was no fool
He knew a trick or two
He learned all he could from God
About following a path that was true

God had warned him before he left
About this journey into matter
That there would be difficulty up ahead
And sometimes pain, during and after

But Maury he did not hesitate
He said "God, thank you for the turn
I'll go down there to do my best
And be happy with what I learn"

God gave his blessing and sent him forth
He said "Go, son, and do your thing
You have much to learn as of this day
And thereafter as you see what life brings

You will find some Souls who are open
But many more who are closed
And these will trouble you, my dear son
Because you'll know they could be arose

When you encounter these fallen angels
Be kind, or at least, be true
Do not dismiss them too readily, My son
They are lonely and know not what to do

You will learn for yourself their troubles
You will feel their pain in your heart
You will reach out often to touch them you see
For that's the work of which you'll take part

Some will listen to you closely
Others may well avert their eyes
Sometimes there will be disappointments
But sometimes there may be surprise

You will not be bored though, that's certain
For this work will enrich and enlarge
All those who come hear your stories
Will be happy they partook of your charge

And you will enjoy their good company
Because they will teach you about you
That being part of your purpose after all
You will be wealthy beyond dreams wild or true

This journey it cannot be forsaken
All must partake of the path
To return to life's former 'glory'
Out of the 'nowhere' of existing wrath

The Heart it has quite a hunger
An appetite that is truly fine
It seeks out nourishment from everywhere
To reconnect itself to the Divine

The Divine is present in all things
But few down there can really see
They have lost their way through sorrow
They have lost their inner key

You are to help them find a way
Back to that center within
For that is where all real treasures lie
And the past is where to begin

So now you know your true purpose son
Your glory will be had in turn
Your wanderings they will take you there
And you'll be glad you chose this return

I cannot offer you much more than that
This journey it knows not any bounds
It will take you out from yourself
Until you can regain former ground

Your purpose there will take you out
And bring you back once again
It may happen that you lose yourself
In the struggle to win your ends

But eventually the Heart knows quite well
Where truth indeed lies hidden
As it finds its way back once more
To that tender sacred place within

Where Love begins and Love leaves off
Is where all need to return
For that is the source of destiny
And that is the place to reclaim

I hope you won't be too lonely, son
I will send you a friend or two
They will help you on this journey called Life
They will help you, to be you

You see my tender-hearted friend
You must travel this path as well
For how are you to teach others you see
If you do not understand their perils

In this fashion you will come to know
What troubles there can be had
What praises and then what luxuries
Can be brought along to be glad

The road of trials need not be long
If you listen to your Heart real soon
For once you connect with the Eternal in you
Your journey will fast become a boon

Now the part that took you through troubled times
Will find itself at a loss
Because the road opening up ahead
Can be taken without a Cross

So when you journey forth my friend
Remember to please look within
For there you will find your truest friend
Your Soul, a gift, from Him

The Love of God will be with you then
Know this to be sure and true
There is no doubt that He knows all
And is with you through and through

Do you understand now, Maury, my friend
What this journey be all about
I need your help in returning to Me
All the Souls that are lost to doubt

They are looking for a star to guide and serve
To bring them out of the night
This star is you, My son, oh yes
I have sent you on a quest that is right

If you happen to find your way back to Me
Before your journey is through
There can be no shame in this return
For you did all that you could do

But if perchance you light the way
For many to find a route Home
We'll be glad you had the best of times
Helping others find a way of their own

That is all, My son, I wanted to say
I hoped that you would understand
If it works out well, then let praise be
We have done the work that was at hand

And in the end you and I will agree
That the journey was well worth the price
For how else could one learn the value of Love
If he did not have its opposite in his life"

This Love we seek is everywhere
And also present deep within
It's where we sprang from when we began
It comes directly from our source that is Him

Let us now end this tale of mercies sought
Let us see what Love hath wrought
Let us hope that He who guides us forth
Is pleased with what we had brought

You will know in the end how your journey has fared
By the mercies that rest in your Heart
For there my friend the tale will be told
And you'll know that you did your part

Amen

Where Eagles Fly

ometimes it is difficult to imagine what is the meaning or significance of one's life or what is one's place in the larger scheme of things. With the Universe being so vast and seemingly complex, it is easier for one to feel lost and insignificant. And yet, when we look more closely at any aspect of life, we begin to see how all of its great and varied forms are intertwined, how even the tiniest of these rely on each other and influence each other in some imperceptible way. From this perspective all expressions of life and energy become meaningful and, without a doubt, even necessary as witness this final story.

Once upon a time, not so long ago, there lived a beautiful golden eagle who loved to soar high up in the heavens above. This eagle felt he was master over all he could see. His vision was sharp and clear and, while soaring high up in the bright blue sky, he felt he could see practically forever.

And then, sadly, the day came when this beautiful golden eagle could no longer fly, no more soaring in the heavens above, no more viewing the spectacular landscapes that had once spread out beneath him.

He had grown old and weary and no longer felt the strength or desire to fly.

Our beautiful golden eagle had now become sad and lonely. He felt he had lost his purpose in life. To do what eagles do had been his purpose and as he could no longer do this he felt lost and afraid.

While he sat there, desolate and alone, a rabbit scurried by. Normally a desirable meal for a healthy eagle, but our eagle could only watch as the rabbit hopped along out of harm's way. Other creatures came and went, and again the eagle could only watch. He was truly sad. He had lost his place in the larger scheme of things. His purpose had been to soar and hunt which he could no longer do. It was only a matter of time before he would eventually perish.

And then the eagle died and his Soul went to heaven. There he was greeted by other eagles who had passed on before him.

"Why are you so sad?" the eagles asked.

"Because in my final days I could no longer do what eagles do. I could no longer soar and hunt," he answered, "and that greatly distressed me."

"We understand," they replied. "We too were full of regret in our final days. We mourned the fact that we could no longer fly or hunt as once we did so easily."

All the eagles nodded in agreement as they acknowledged this truth to each other. They too looked very sad and forlorn.

"But is that not life?" announced a voice from far in the rear of the group. "Is that not the nature of being an eagle? You are born, you learn to fly, you soar high up into the heavens and you hunt. Is that not the essence of eagle life? And when you no longer can do this, when your time to soar and hunt is over, you pass out of that realm and come into this one. Is that not simply the cycle of life?"

All the eagles began to mumble amongst themselves, pondering what had just been shared, and then they started looking around to see who had spoken. There, in the back of the group, where all of them could now clearly see, stood a proud and powerful figure, an eagle of unusual proportions and stature, more beautiful than any of them had ever seen, and with a special glow all around her that seemed to sparkle whenever she moved or spoke.

"Who are you?" they asked in unison.

"I am the Master Eagle from heaven," She replied. "I am the Eagle of eagles. I am the one who guided you when you were in flight and when you were on the hunt. I am your guardian, your protector and your source of inspiration for eagle life while you were on the Earth plane. And it is I who bid you to return to Me when your time down there has ended. Do you not recall hearing my voice as you soared in the heavens, directing you, nudging you along, encouraging you to try your very best? Do you not recall my whispers in the night as you slept away that day's fatigue? I have been your friend and your guide throughout your life. I have always been with you."

All the eagles nodded in agreement. They truly had heard and felt these things but did not know at the time from where these sensations came. They had all assumed it was simply part of being an eagle and had never questioned the source of their inspiration or guidance.

"We see," they said in unison. "You are the one who guided us throughout our lives."

"That is correct," she replied, "I am the One."

The newest arrival from the eagle group stepped forward and exclaimed, "You are that voice that I heard in my head and felt in my heart.

You taught me to fly and to hunt. You taught me how to be an eagle. I recognize you now. How wonderful you look in full view."

"Thank you," the Master Eagle replied. "That is indeed who I am."

"So it is not such a sad thing to be called to heaven?" the new arrival then asked.

"Of course not," the Master Eagle continued. "You have done what you were expected to do. You learned to fly, you soared and you hunted. That is what eagles do and you did it well."

"Thank you," he replied. "Thank you for helping me understand that my life was truly full and meaningful after all."

"You are most welcome," she replied. And then she proceeded to move out from the center of the group.

All the eagles gathered around to continue the conversation. They talked at length about eagle life and eagle purpose. They all began to realize that they too had done well. Each of them in their own way had learned important lessons and made a valuable contribution to eagle life and all life around them. They had done well indeed. It seemed impossible to notice at the time, but there was no doubt now that this was in fact true. Each of their lives while on the Earth plane had been important and valuable. Each of them had contributed in their own unique way.

All the eagles now seemed quite happy with this realization and their newest arrival was also pleased. He was prepared now to accept his fate and could see the value in his final sufferings. He too had made an important contribution to eagle life while he flew and soared in the Earth's beautiful blue skies. He felt satisfied with that realization. No more tears, no more sorrow, he had done his very best.

"Now on to other things," the Master Eagle shouted out as she proceeded to move toward a new horizon that had just now come into view. "You have new worlds to conquer, new lessons to learn, new spaces in which to fly and soar. Rejoice and be pleased with yourselves, and know that what I have said to you is true." And they did, and they knew:

That All Was Truly Well in Their World

There are those who cry from out the night
Their hearts ablaze, their minds in fright
Do they know now what fears they tread?
Do they know ever what is they dread?
With gazes fixed upon that "tree"
Does it become the place that's free?
To all about, concerns and doubts
Have no place here, inside or out

All out there are prepared to leave
This heart behind, too broken and cleaved
Separated from its one true Source
Can it be led back onto its course?
The answer heard is here at last
Can take one back to their true path
Find your Heart, your Self, your Soul
Find all of these and then be bold

About the Author

Maurice J. Turmel Ph.D. is a therapist in private practice in Winnipeg, Manitoba, Canada. For the past 21 years Dr. Turmel has been exploring the various therapeutic modalities that can facilitate growth. More recently this interest has expanded to include the world of Mythology. Here Dr. Turmel has found a framework with which to convey positive messages about dealing with pain, working through personal issues, and growing to one's full potential by actualizing the Self and then connecting with one's Soul. Self and Soul are now his main areas of exploration. Through the use of Mythical stories and poetry Dr. Turmel likes to focus on the essence of one's spiritual journey which, he believes, must include both the emotional and psychological dimensions of being. This is his first book of "mythical tales" and a follow up is underway. He also enjoys writing children's stories and a collection of these is forthcoming as well.

He and his wife, Leslee, live in the country where they like to be close to nature. They have two daughters, three grandchildren and their faithful companion "Sam".

Dr. Turmel has been conducting seminars and workshops on *Awakening the Soul* using stories and guided meditations from this book and his upcoming book "Parables from the Cradle". To set up a workshop in your area please contact the publishers.

LightWing Publishing
392 Academy Road, Suite "C"
Winnipeg, Manitoba, Canada
R3N 0B8
(204) 489 - 2756

Coming soon from LightWing Publishing

Winter 95/96

𝔓arables from the 𝔠radle

by
Maurice Turmel

The much anticipated follow up to "*Mythical Times*", Dr. Turmel continues with his mythical themes of exploring the Self, with a specific purpose. The stories and poetry in this book are an inspired "Call to Arms" for all seekers on the Spiritual path. With pageantry and a sense of purpose he reaches into our Souls to show us why we are here and to encourage us to express our own essence. Beautifully illustrated by Monica Yakiwchuk.

Spring/96

𝔐essages from the 𝔉airy 𝔓rincess

by
Maurice Turmel

A compilation of children's stories with spiritual and mythical themes designed to stimulate the young reader to explore his or her spirituality. The Fairy Princess serves as a guide to this process by taking the reader on a number of journeys, each with a purpose of engaging them into discovering their spiritual heritage. For children of all ages. Adults will enjoy these stories as well. Beautifully illustrated by Monica Yakiwchuk.

Ordering Information

Additional copies of *Mythical Times* are available through the Publisher.

Also available: *Heroic Journeys*, Guided Meditation and Relaxation Tape.
- ✝ Narrated by Maurice Turmel
- ✝ Solo piano and nature soundtrack by recording artist Ken Johnson

Side A - Journey of Discovery:
A fanciful romp toward a magical mountain with a host of mythical characters along the way.

Side B - Journey into Healing:
A gentle and soothing "light" bath designed to take You away from it all.

Special quantity discounts are available for Books and/or Tapes:
- ✝ 10% OFF for 10 or more items   ✝ 20% OFF for 20 or more items
- ✝ 50 or more items, please call for a quote.

To order the above items write to:

LightWing Publishing
392 Academy Road, Suite "C"
Winnipeg, Manitoba, Canada, R3N 0B8

Or call your order in to: (204) 489 - 2756
Visa/MasterCard orders welcomed

SHIPPING & HANDLING: please add $2.00 for the first item and $1.00 for each additional item. Canadian residents add 7% GST.

Name _____

Address _____

Province/State _____

Postal Code/Zip _____

Item	Price	Quantity	Sub-Total
"Mythical Times" Book	$18.95 CAN	_____	
	$15.95 US	_____	
"Heroic Journeys" Tape	$12.00 CAN	_____	
	$10.00 US	_____	

(Discount) _____

Shipping/Handling _____

GST _____

TOTAL Enclosed _____